"I'm scared."

Cooper nodded, and he reached out. Took her by the arm and pulled her to him.

Almost immediately, she felt him stiffen, and he no doubt would have stepped away from her if Jessa hadn't caught on to him. Why, she didn't know.

Okay, she did.

It was because that brief moment in his arms had felt darn good. Reassuring. And safe. She hadn't felt safe in days, but it was a mistake to look for that safety in Cooper's arms. And the sound that rumbled in his throat let her know that he agreed.

But he didn't move.

Neither did she.

Jessa just stood there with one of his arms hooked around her. Their gazes met. Held. And she felt that tug again. The one deep in her belly that she didn't want to feel.

This is not going to happen between us," she reminded him, and herself. "It can't."

MAVERICK SHERIFF

USA TODAY Bestselling Author

DELORES FOSSEN

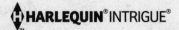

Recycling programs
for this product may
not exist in your area.

ISBN-13: 978-0-373-74836-5

MAVERICK SHERIFF

Copyright © 2014 by Delores Fossen

Printed in U.S.A.

ABOUT THE AUTHOR

Imagine a family tree that includes Texas cowboys, Choctaw and Cherokee Indians, a Louisiana pirate and a Scottish rebel who battled side by side with William Wallace. With ancestors like that, it's easy to understand why *USA TODAY* bestselling author and former air force captain Delores Fossen feels as if she were genetically predisposed to writing romances. Along the way to fulfilling her DNA destiny, Delores married an air force top gun who just happens to be of Viking descent. With all those romantic bases covered, she doesn't have to look too far for inspiration.

Books by Delores Fossen

HARLEQUIN INTRIGUE

CAST OF CHARACTERS

Sheriff Cooper McKinnon—This cowboy lawman learns that his missing son could not only be alive but also illegally adopted by the district attorney who's just charged his mother with murder.

Jessa Wells—All she's ever wanted to be is a mom, and now her precious son is at risk. To keep him safe, she must trust Cooper, the very man who could take him from her.

Liam Wells—Jessas two-year-old adopted son.

Hector Dixon—The attorney who handled Liam's adoption. He could be trying to cover his tracks, or someone could be setting him up.

Peggy Dawes—A baby broker who claims to match adoptive parents with babies, but she might have participated in some illegal adoptions.

Donovan Bradfield—This cattle baron and Cooper are longtime enemies, but how far would he go to right what he believes to be an old wrong?

Chapter One

The moment Sheriff Cooper McKinnon stepped through the hospital's emergency room doors, he spotted the woman running toward him. Not hurrying.

Flat-out running.

He'd only known the running woman, Jessa Wells, for a few months now. Since she'd moved to Sweetwater Springs to take the job as the town's assistant district attorney. A move that continued to be a thorn in Cooper's professional and personal sides.

Like the woman herself.

But that wasn't a thorny look she was giving Cooper now. She was a mess.

Her light brown hair was tangled on her shoulders, and there were small nicks and cuts on her face. White powder from a car's deployed air bag was clinging like dust to her already pale gray skirt and top. Everything about her expression was an emotion he knew all too well.

Fear.

Remembering that fear, and the panic, it felt as if someone had just punched him in the gut. *Mercy.* Despite his feelings about Jessa, Cooper prayed her situation turned out better than his.

One lost child was enough.

"Hurry," Jessa insisted, catching his arm and practically dragging him out of the E.R. waiting room and into a side corridor. "Dr. Howland's ready to draw your blood."

She was ashy pale—the only spots of color were those wide blue eyes. Desperate eyes.

Yet something else Cooper understood.

"It's my son," she said, though he didn't know how she managed to speak with her breath gusting like that. She was dragging in air through her mouth at a much too fast rate.

"Yeah. When the doctor called me, he said your boy, Liam, was two years old and that he'd been hurt."

Jessa managed a shaky nod. "We were in a car accident. Someone sideswiped me." She gave a hoarse groan. "And his spleen ruptured. I didn't even know that could happen to a toddler."

Lots of bad things could happen to babies and toddlers, and Cooper wished he didn't know that firsthand.

She threw open the door to an examining room. Not an empty one, but there was no sign

f her son inside. Just Dr. Howland, his nurse
Tammy Karnes and a table set up for Cooper to
give blood.

Other than the panicked mother and the feeling
of urgency, this was familiar ground for Cooper,
since Dr. Howland often called him to donate
blood. This was a first, however—a child who
might literally die without it.

"Thanks for coming so fast," Dr. Howland
greeted.

The doc looked every day of his sixty-plus
years this morning. Heaven knew how many life-
and-death situations like this he'd faced over his
long career as a small-town doctor. How many
babies he'd delivered.

And saved.

Heck, he'd delivered Cooper and his two brothers and had saved them a time or two over their
years as law enforcement officers. He hoped the
doc could do the same for Jessa's little boy.

Cooper took off his Stetson and got on the
table, his belt holster and gun clattering against
the metal side. The nurse didn't waste any time
swabbing his finger. All routine. She jabbed it
to get the drops of blood that she needed for a
quick test to make sure he wasn't too anemic to
donate. While she scurried away to do that, the
doctor rubbed his arm with antiseptic and in-
serted the needle.

The wait began.

It wouldn't be long, but it would no doubt seem like a lifetime to Jessa. She stood at the end of the table, her gaze firing all around, mumbling a prayer under her breath.

The door flew open and the nurse hurried back in. "We're good to go."

That was the only green light the doctor needed, because he turned on the machine and got Cooper's blood flowing into the collection bag. It seemed the doctor was collecting a lot for a toddler, but maybe it was necessary if Jessa's son had lost a lot of blood.

"I was so thankful when Dr. Howland told me you were a match for Liam," Jessa said.

Or rather that was what she tried to say. Her voice cracked, and that too-fast breath caught up with her. Obviously it'd made her light-headed, and she wobbled enough for the doctor to reach out and take hold of her. Dr. Howland tried to move her to the chair in the corner of the room, but Jessa frantically shook her head and stayed put.

"We're lucky," the doctor added. "AB negative is the rarest blood type."

What the doctor didn't say was what he'd told Cooper when he called him. That if Cooper hadn't been nearby, just up the street at the sheriff's office, then Jessa's son would have had a much slimmer chance of pulling through this injury.

"I know you hate me," Jessa mumbled. She blinked, but there were no tears. They would no doubt come once the shock wore off. "But thank you for doing this. *Thank you.*"

Cooper didn't disagree with the hate part, though he probably should have tried to play nice. But he couldn't. Jessa was in shock and panicky now, but the bottom line was that she was trying to destroy his family. And him specifically.

Too bad she was doing it legally.

"I heard your mother's coming back to town," Dr. Howland tossed out there, casting an uneasy glance first at Jessa. Then at Cooper. The nurse, Tammy Karnes, made some uneasy glances of her own.

Because this was a powder keg of a subject. One that Cooper couldn't dodge since he was confined to the table with a captive audience. However, he didn't have to blab his head off about the details, either.

"Yeah, she's coming back," Cooper confirmed. Jewell McKinnon was indeed returning to Sweetwater Springs after being gone for twenty-three years.

It would *not* be a happy homecoming, and that was a massive understatement.

"Well, I'll try to get you out of here as fast as

I can," the doctor assured him. "So you can be home when she arrives."

"No need for fast." Cooper didn't have a firm time for his mother's arrival, and nobody in his immediate family was pushing for one. Not even Jewell herself, since she was trying to make travel arrangements not just for Cooper's twin sisters but also for her stepson.

For support, no doubt.

Good thing, too, since Jewell wasn't likely to get any support from the now ex-husband and the three sons she'd abandoned.

Including Cooper.

"Besides," Cooper went on, "Jessa here has plans to have Jewell hauled off to jail as soon as her feet land on Sweetwater Springs's soil. She'd have me hauled off, too, if she could ever find proof that I stonewalled this investigation and tampered with evidence. Since I didn't do those things, there's no proof for her to find."

"Someone tampered with that crime scene and the box of evidence," she mumbled.

Yeah. Someone had. Cooper had seen the photos, and someone had tried to do a cleanup. But it sure as heck hadn't been him. He'd been just a kid at the time of that crime scene.

As for the evidence, well, there was something missing, all right, including the collection log. So they didn't even know what'd been taken.

Again, not his doing.

"I figure Jewell will go straight to the county sheriff's office and just turn herself in to the deputy there," Cooper clarified. At least that was what he was hoping she'd do, so it would prevent Cooper and his family from having to deal with her.

For the time being, anyway.

Jessa nodded, and despite the terror that she was no doubt feeling, he could see her slip into her assistant district attorney mode. "Your mother murdered a man, and even though the body wasn't found, there's enough evidence left to confirm it was murder. She has to pay for that."

Yes, there was enough evidence. *Blood.* Fitting, since that was what had brought him to Jessa today. It could save a life, but with the large quantities found at the crime scene, it meant the loss of life.

In this case, it did indeed mean murder.

That wouldn't have concerned him so much if the murder charges hadn't brought Jewell back into their lives. Where the old wounds and memories would rip at his whole family. Especially his father, who could end up being implicated in his old crime, as well. He could thank Jessa for that and her vendetta-like investigation that had brought them to this.

Well, not to the hospital.

No way had she counted on something like this interfering with her plans to arrest a woman for a twenty-three-year-old murder.

"Ironic, huh?" Cooper said, looking at Jessa. "Of all the blood in Texas, your son's had to match mine?"

"Yes," Jessa quietly agreed. No more professional facade. "I wish I'd matched, but I didn't. And there wasn't time to try to track down his birth parents. Liam needs a transfusion now." She paused, shook her head. "I'm sorry if this brings back any bad memories for you."

They weren't talking about Jewell now but his late son, Cameron. Something Cooper damn sure didn't want to discuss with Jessa. But he'd never had any luck fighting back those bad memories.

He didn't have luck with it now, either.

As his blood flowed into the bag, the memories flowed, too. First of the storm nearly two years ago. Such a small, ordinary thing that'd had life-changing consequences. His wife, Molly, had driven Cameron into town for his six-week checkup and his shots. Molly had been dreading those. Cooper, too. He'd planned to meet them at the clinic so they could hold each other's hands and get through yet something else that was supposed to be routine.

Then the storm got worse.

The floodwaters came.

And in the exact moment that Molly's car had reached the Stone Creek bridge, it'd washed out.

Taking Cameron and Molly with it.

Cooper squeezed his eyes shut, trying to push away the images. Finally, he gave up and let them bash at him like angry waves, punching into him until he wasn't sure if it was blood or ice being drawn from him.

He hadn't been able to say goodbye to his son. Hadn't been able to bury him. Because his body had never been found.

Unlike Molly's.

Her lifeless body had been found in the creek. Now she had a grave with an empty space next to it, and there were days, like now, when Cooper had to fight hard not to wish he was in that ground beside her.

"Done," the nurse said, and Dr. Howland took the blood bags and hurried out. Jessa was right behind him.

The nurse eased the needle from his arm and positioned a bandage over the puncture before she attempted to help Cooper to his feet. But he waved her off. He'd never gotten dizzy after a donation, and the only thing he wanted to do was get the heck out of there.

Of course, that meant making plans to face Jewell, her stepson and Cooper's fraternal twin sisters, whom Jewell had taken with her when she left the ranch. Funny that seeing his estranged mother now seemed a better option than staying here with these memories eating away at him.

Cooper pulled down his shirtsleeve and went out the door, only to find Jessa there, pacing and looking ready to explode.

"Dr. Howland said I had to wait here," she blurted out.

Man, her voice was trembling all over, and for a moment he considered offering her a shoulder, but then he thought better of it. With their bad feelings for each other, even a genuine shoulder offer would seem hollow.

"Once your boy gets the blood, he should be all right," Cooper told her. It wasn't much of a reassurance. Heck, it might not even be true, but it was something he would have wanted her to say to him if their situations had been reversed.

"I can't do this." She was past the frantic stage now, and the tears came.

Oh, mercy.

He really didn't want to deal with this, and looked around for someone to take over comfort duty. Of course, there was no one else. Any other day, there would have been all sorts of people milling around. But apparently the fates had it in for Jessa and him today.

"Where's your son?" Cooper asked, hoping

that by talking she wouldn't shatter into a million little pieces. It'd worked in the collection room when she had slipped into her district attorney mode for a couple of seconds.

She pointed to the room behind her. Surgery. Well, that explained why Jessa hadn't been allowed in.

"How strong's your stomach?" he asked.

Jessa blinked, clearly not expecting him to ask that. "At the moment not very strong, but if you're asking if I want to see my son in surgery, I do."

He was afraid she'd say that, but since he had already walked out on this limb, Cooper kept right on walking. He led her farther down the hall and into a room with a set of stairs.

"There's an observation deck," he explained. "They bring in medical students sometimes."

And sometimes he'd used it to check on the status of a perp or a victim who'd been injured. Cooper had stood right in that very spot to watch Doc Howland dig a bullet from his brother's chest. That had turned out all right.

Maybe the same would happen today.

Maybe.

Jessa hurried to the glass, her breath instantly fogging it. Her son was indeed on the table, though Cooper couldn't see much of him because of the green sea of scrubs surrounding him. Cooper's blood was there, already flowing into the boy.

Man, he looked so little.

Hardly more than a baby.

"The surgeon seems to be finishing up," Cooper told her. "Everything looks good."

Well, the machines were all beeping and doing the right thing. That had to be good. Ditto for the fact that no one appeared to be in panic mode. Except for Jessa, that was. Even Dr. Howland was standing near the surgeon, just calmly watching.

"I can never thank you enough," she repeated.

And just like that, she came at him, and despite how he felt about the woman, it was the terrified mother whom he put his arms around.

"You don't have to thank me." Cooper tried to ease her away, but she stayed put. Pressed against him.

This wasn't a man-woman thing, but maybe because he was so raw from the memories, he got another punch of feelings that he didn't want to have. Jessa was attractive, and his stupid body didn't let him overlook that. When Cooper felt that too-familiar curl of heat go through him, he untangled himself from her and stepped back.

Way back.

Getting involved with a convicted felon would cause him less trouble than getting involved with this woman.

Jessa didn't seem shocked that he'd pushed her away. Only a little embarrassed that she'd sought out comfort from him in the first place. She snapped back to the window, her gaze fastened to her son.

"What are the odds that you'd be here right when Liam needed you?" he heard her say.

A different kind of uneasy feeling went through him.

Yeah, what were the odds?

Cooper tried to stop any crazy thoughts from flying through his head, but he failed at that, too. He was failing at a lot of things today.

"How old did you say your son is?" he asked.

"Two."

"And his birthday?"

The sharp look Jessa gave him made him wish he'd used a little more tact in asking that question. A stupid question. Because her son had nothing to do with Cameron.

"March 3," she finally said.

Cameron had been born on February 27 of that same year. So it was close, but not the same.

Not that it would have mattered if it had been.

His son had washed away in the flood. His son, with the same rare type of blood as Cooper had.

And Jessa's adopted son.

Less than six percent of world's population had that blood type, and no one else in the county that he knew about. Even his brothers had dodged the rare-blood-type bullet that Cooper had managed to get from a bad combination of Jewell's B-negative and his father's A-positive blood.

Cameron, however, had inherited it.

That uneasy feeling got worse.

Cooper couldn't stop himself. He moved to the glass, stepping all the way to the side until he could get a look at the little boy.

There was an oxygen mask on his face, but it didn't conceal his forehead. Or his hair.

Oh, mercy.

The uneasy feeling slammed into him like a Mack truck.

That was the shape of Cooper's forehead. The color of his hair.

And even though it didn't make sense, Cooper had to wonder if he might be looking at the son he'd thought he had lost.

God, was that Cameron?

Chapter Two

Jessa didn't know what had caused that bleached-out look to appear on Cooper's face, and she wasn't sure she wanted the answer. Something about this just wasn't right.

But then, how could it be?

Cooper had saved her son, and yet she and the sheriff were basically enemies. On opposite sides of the law, and it didn't help that he was the top lawman who ran this town. Heck, one of his brothers was the deputy and another was a Texas Ranger, making this a situation of her against an entire family of testosterone-heavy, badge-wearing cowboys.

Even now, with her mind a tornado of emotions, that bothered her.

Cooper and his brothers could be manipulating evidence, and no telling what else to shelter their father from the fallout of a crime their mother had committed. Jessa was actually thankful for that aggravating reminder.

Because it was better than thinking about what was going on below them in surgery.

It broke her heart for her baby to be here on that operating table. Maybe in pain. And with no certain outcome. Yes, the doctor had said he'd be okay. Cooper had said it, too. But Jessa wouldn't believe it until she could hold Liam in her arms again.

The tears came again, though she tried her best to blink them back. They tumbled down her cheeks, and this time Cooper didn't move to pull her into his arms.

Good thing, too.

Everything inside her was tangled into one giant, raw nerve, and she didn't need to be leaning on this man.

"Will you call his birth parents and let them know what happened?" Cooper asked.

"No." It took her a moment to pull herself out of her thoughts and fears to answer him. "It was a private adoption. The records are sealed." She paused, noted his weird expression again. "Why do you ask?"

He lifted his shoulder in what was probably meant to be a casual shrug, but that wasn't a casual look in his eyes. "I just wondered what would happen if he needed more blood. They won't let me donate any more for a while."

Sweet heaven. She hadn't considered that.

Cooper and she were at odds, but his blood had saved her baby's life. And she might have to ask him to do it again.

But what if he couldn't?

Since she suddenly felt as if her legs might give way, Jessa groped behind her to locate one of the metal chairs and dropped down into it. "Liam has to be all right. He's all I have."

"Yeah." And with just that one word, she heard the old scars that had created this dark and brooding lawman. "There are other donors out there with my blood type. None in this area, but Dr. Howland's probably already put out the call to make sure he has enough blood on hand."

That helped. Well, as much as a basic reassurance could help. The only thing that would truly get her through this was having her baby well.

"Keep talking," Cooper insisted. "They're doing all they can do for your boy, and for his sake, you can't fall apart."

He was right, but Jessa thought she would explode if the surgery didn't end now. God, how did other mothers handle this? It seemed impossible.

Cooper buttoned the cuff on his dark blue shirt and eased down next to her.

Not directly next to her, though.

He put his cocoa-brown Stetson in the seat between them. Only then did she realize she'd never seen him without the hat that was nearly the same color as his hair. The Stetson had seemed like part of his cowboy-cop uniform—like his boots, badge and jeans.

Yet another thing that was off.

He had on the other *uniform* items, but without that Stetson on his head, he no longer looked like the formidable lawman she'd been battling for weeks.

As if to anchor his hands in place, he hooked his thumbs over the belt holster that held both his gun and his badge. What he didn't do was take his attention off her son.

"Why'd you go the adoption route?" he asked.

Jessa kept her attention plastered to Liam, too, and tried to tamp down her breathing. "You mean there's something you don't know about me? I figured you had run a thorough background check by now."

"Oh, I have. I know you're thirty-three. Divorced. And you were an assistant D.A. one county over before you moved here. Nothing in that background check said why you adopted."

No. It wouldn't. Résumés and records didn't reveal a need so deep that she'd ached for it. "Because I wanted a child, and I figured there were plenty of children out there who needed a parent."

Besides, she'd given up on finding Mr. Right to help her make a baby and a family. There'd been too many Mr. Wrongs in her life for her to keep believing that particular fantasy, and she hadn't wanted an unfulfilled fantasy to get in the way of what she wanted most—motherhood.

"It's funny," she added. "But just this week I requested information about Liam's birth parents. You know, family history stuff in case something like this happened. If I'd gotten the info sooner, I would have known about his rare blood type. I could have told the doctor straight off and it wouldn't have wasted precious minutes."

"They still would have had to test him," Cooper assured her. "They can't go pumping blood into somebody without confirming the type."

True. But Jessa couldn't help but think that she could have done more. Every second had been critical, and she prayed those lost seconds hadn't hurt her son's chances of making a full recovery.

"How'd this car accident happen?" Cooper asked. "You said someone sideswiped you?"

Jessa certainly hadn't forgotten about the accident that had brought them here. In fact, she would press Cooper for a thorough investigation later, but it was hard to remember the details with all these emotions cutting through her. Still, she tried. Best to tell him before she forgot anything.

"I was on Silver Mine Road, less than a mile from my house, and this truck came out of nowhere. The driver must have been on one of those old ranch trails because he pulled out right behind me. He was going so fast and tried to pass. That's when he hit my car, and I went into the ditch. He stopped for just a second or two, but then this other car came, and the driver of the truck sped off."

Thankfully, the other driver, Herman Hendricks, a rancher who owned the property not far from hers, had called the ambulance right away.

Cooper made a sound to indicate he was thinking about what she'd said. "And you didn't get the truck's license plate number?"

She shook her head. "I barely had time to think. The air bags deployed, even the one in the back where I had Liam strapped into his car seat." The guilt tore through her, and she had to choke back a sob.

"This is my fault," she managed to say. "Liam's favorite toy is this hard plastic horse, and I let him hold it while he was in the car seat. The air bag must have hit the horse, and that's what ruptured his spleen."

Cooper huffed. "Even if that's what happened, you had no way of knowing that some fool would force you off the road." He paused. "Did you recognize the truck?"

Another head shake. "And I wasn't really looking for side traffic. I mean, there's usually no one else on that part of the road at that time of morning. It was a miracle Mr. Hendricks was there."

She'd allowed herself to be lulled into a false sense of safety. And she'd desperately wanted safe. That was why she'd moved her son to the small rural house three miles outside of town.

Cooper looked ready to launch into more questions, but his phone buzzed. He stretched out his jeans-clad leg so he could take it from his pocket. They were close, practically shoulder to shoulder despite the seat with his Stetson between them, so she could see the name on the screen.

Colt McKinnon.

His brother, the deputy.

Cooper didn't put the call on speaker, but it was impossible for her to miss what Colt said in the otherwise soundless room. "Jewell and the others are coming in the day after tomorrow. They're not going straight to the county sheriff's office, though. They're coming out to the ranch."

His mouth tightened. "Why the hell are they going there?"

Colt didn't answer right away. "Dad asked her that, and Jewell reminded him that she owns the ranch. Not him. Not us."

Jessa hadn't thought it possible, but Cooper's mouth tightened even more.

The ranch's ownership wasn't a surprise. She knew that Jewell owned it outright, an inheritance from her own grandfather before she'd married Roy McKinnon. But Jessa was surprised the woman would play the ownership card when she had to know she wouldn't be welcome there.

"Jewell wants the guesthouse fixed up for her stepson and the twins," Colt added. "She says they'll be staying there while she's awaiting trial."

Jessa silently groaned. Oh, mercy. Cooper's mother was really pushing it hard. Even though her daughters were Cooper's full-blooded siblings, Jessa had heard that he hadn't seen them since they were kids. Thankfully, Jewell wouldn't be bringing her second husband, since he'd passed away years ago. Still, it'd be a mess since it would no doubt be months before the trial even started.

"What about the arresting officer?" Cooper asked. "Will he come out to the ranch for her?"

Cooper said *arresting officer* as if it were some kind of bug to be squashed. She hadn't expected a different reaction. Nor had Jessa had a choice in requesting someone from outside of Sweetwater Springs. She couldn't expect Jewell's own sons to make the arrest. The FBI was out, too, since Jewell's stepson was an agent. Ditto for the Rangers, because Cooper's brother was one.

That left the county sheriff, but that was a conflict of interest, too, since the county sheriff's father was the very man Jewell was accused of murdering. That was why Jessa had gotten permission from the state attorney general for a county deputy to do the deed. Hardly in the county deputy's job description to make an arrest for a murder in a town that had an entire law enforcement team, but it seemed the best alternative considering the circumstances.

"Are you out at the accident scene where the A.D.A. was run off the road?" Cooper asked.

"Yeah. No skid marks, but I can see the point of impact on her car where she was sideswiped."

"Look for tracks on the ranch trail several yards before the impact. Jessa says that's where the truck came out."

Cooper had used her given name, but he hadn't said it with any kind of affection. In fact, it'd seemed to stick in his throat, but it would have seemed petty to call her Ms. Wells after she'd launched herself into his arms earlier.

Something Jessa already regretted.

No sense breaking down the kinds of barriers that needed to stay in place.

"How's her boy?" she heard Colt ask.

Since Cooper's gaze was still on her son, he had a quick answer. "Surgery's finishing up now."

"You okay?" Colt said after pausing.

"Fine." Cooper jabbed the end-call button so hard she was surprised his phone didn't shatter.

Like her.

The panic was boiling through her again, and since it did indeed seem as if the surgery was wrapping up, she headed for the stairs. Cooper followed. Well, he ambled along behind her anyway, and caught up with her when she stopped outside the operating room doors.

She wanted to burst into the room, to beg for any information anyone could give her, but being closer to Liam didn't lessen the panic. It only made it worse.

Jessa started pacing.

"You should go," she said to Cooper. Though she didn't want him to leave. Yes, it was crazy, but he might be the only person nearby who actually knew what she was going through.

"I got a few minutes." Though he did check the time on his phone. "I need to do some paperwork, but it can wait."

There wasn't as much venom in his voice as she'd expected. Especially considering the massive amount of venom that'd been between them since she'd requested the county sheriff reopen this investigation.

"You think I'm on a witch hunt to have your mother arrested," she said. She didn't want to have this discussion with him, but after what he'd done for her and Liam, Jessa wanted to give him an explanation.

Well, as much as she could give, anyway.

Cooper already knew about the forensics. He'd no doubt studied every last detail. Twenty-three years ago, there'd been enough of Whitt Braddock's blood found in a hunting cabin on the grounds of his massive ranch for him to be declared dead, despite the fact his body was missing.

Dragged from the cabin, from the looks of it.

Rumors were rampant that Whitt and Jewell had been having an affair, and that she'd killed him in the heat of passion when he'd tried to break things off with her and go back to his wife. The rumors had stayed just that.

Rumors.

Until Jessa had arrived in town as the new A.D.A., and she'd requested items taken from the old crime scene be tested. Jewell's DNA had been discovered on both the bed sheets and the knife that'd been found near the scene.

"I'm just sorry your mother's the target of my investigation," she added.

Cooper spared her a hard glance. "It's not my mother I'm worried about. She can take care of herself."

There it was. The venom. It wasn't aimed at her but rather his mother. Of course, Jewell had abandoned her husband and sons when she'd fled town under a cloud of suspicion. Cooper, his brothers and his father had to resent that, and it showed in his voice.

The door behind her finally opened, and Jessa turned so fast that her neck popped. It was Dr. Howland, and even though she'd never been happier to see someone, she couldn't read his expression.

He tugged the surgical mask off his mouth and nodded. "Liam's going to be okay."

The relief was instant, flooding through her and turning her legs to mush. If Cooper hadn't taken hold of her arm, she probably would have just crumpled to the floor.

Maybe sensing that Cooper wasn't exactly comfortable with rescue detail, the doctor took over. "Come on. They're moving him to the recovery room soon, and you can see him."

Despite everything feeling wobbly, Jessa got herself walking. She could see her little boy and make sure for herself that he was indeed okay. Thankfully, she didn't have to go far. Just two doors down, and Dr. Howland opened it for her and ushered her inside. Liam wasn't there yet, and she prayed she didn't have to wait much longer.

"I'll be back in a minute," the doctor told her, and stepped into the hall where Cooper was still waiting.

"All right, what's wrong?" she heard the doctor ask him.

Puzzled, Jessa stayed in the doorway, peering around the side, and she tried to hear Cooper's response. But he just shook his head and mumbled something she didn't catch.

Maybe this was about his late wife and child. Maybe the ordeal had brought back bad memories. Of course, the sheriff was about to face a whole boatload of new bad memories thanks to his mother and Jessa's investigation.

Since this was likely a very private conversation, Jessa started to move away so she wouldn't be able to hear. Then Cooper pulled in a hard breath and turned to the side so that she couldn't see his expression. But she could tell from his body language that whatever was bothering him wasn't good.

"I need you to run a DNA test," Cooper said to the doctor. She missed whatever he added to the request.

DNA? So maybe this wasn't personal. Maybe it had something to do with a case. Except she knew all of his investigations, and there wasn't one that required any kind of DNA test.

"I can get a court order," Cooper went on. "Or we can do this quietly. For now. If anything turns up, then I'd have to make it official, of course."

The doctor didn't say anything for several moments and shook his head. "I'm afraid you'll need that court order for this."

If Cooper had a reaction to that, she couldn't see it. He simply nodded. "You'll have it within the hour. Then I want the test done ASAP."

"Sure. Once I have the order." Dr. Howland paused again. "Whose DNA are we comparing to his?"

Cooper turned and delivered his answer from over his shoulder. "Mine."

Chapter Three

Cooper's mind wasn't where it darn well should be. Even two days after donating blood, his thoughts were still on the little boy, Liam, at the hospital. The boy who now had Cooper's blood in his veins.

He'd already made at least a dozen calls to find out his condition. The boy was recovering, something Dr. Howland kept saying every time Cooper asked. That was good. But it wasn't the same as seeing Liam.

Or knowing the truth about his paternity.

It was such a long shot that this boy could be his son. But after living with no shot at all for nearly two years, Cooper had grabbed on to the sliver of hope as if it were a lifeline.

But it was a lifeline that he had to push aside.

Because all hell was about to break loose.

He'd had to make a lot of waves to get that court order for the DNA test, and by now half the county had probably heard about his request, or rumors of it, anyway.

Including Jessa.

She hadn't contacted him about it yet, which meant by some miracle she hadn't heard or either she was still too worried about Liam to do anything about it.

Cooper was worried, too. For the boy. For this blasted hope that he couldn't tamp down. For the test result that he should have in the next twenty-four hours or sooner.

And worried for what the coming days would bring with Jewell's arrival.

Unfortunately, he couldn't push the latter aside because it was driving up the ranch road directly for the house he called home.

"Figured she'd be driving something flashier than that," his kid brother, Colt, mumbled. He had his attention fixed to the white car that was kicking up a trail of dust as it made its way to the house.

Cooper hadn't given a thought to the kind of vehicle. Only the occupants inside. Judging from the way his brother Tucker grunted, he'd done the same.

The three of them stood, shoulder to shoulder, with Cooper in the middle, Tucker on his right, Colt on his left. They'd all worn their badges, holsters and guns. But then, they were rarely without them. Same with the Stetsons, though Colt's and his were dark brown. Since Tucker was a Texas Ranger, his was white.

Cooper hoped they looked intimidating as hell.

Because the last thing he wanted was Jewell and the kids she'd raised on the very land that he, his brothers and dad had worked while Jewell had been off enjoying her life with her second husband.

"Not sure I'll even recognize her," Colt added.

Yeah, because he'd been only nine when she'd walked out twenty-three years ago. Just a kid. Heck, Tucker had only been eleven and Cooper thirteen, but he hadn't been able to get the image of her out of his head.

The image of her leaving.

Her exit and the affair she'd had with Whitt Braddock had crushed his dad, and because of all the pain she had caused, Cooper had made sure any good memories of her were gone, too.

Now here they were.

Right smack-dab in their faces.

"That's her, huh?" Cooper heard the woman say.

It was Arlene Litton, the weathered-faced horse trainer who'd been with them as long as Cooper could remember. Wearing dusty jeans and a plaid shirt that'd seen much better days, she clomped up the side steps of the porch that stretched across the entire bottom floor of the two-story house and joined them.

"You boys okay?" she asked, sounding more like a mother than their horse trainer.

None of them attempted to lie. They weren't okay, and they wouldn't be until Jewell was behind bars. Not until all their names were cleared. And not until Jewell's *kin* was off the ranch.

"When's the county deputy gonna be here to arrest Jewell?" Arlene asked.

"Hopefully any minute," Tucker answered.

Cooper echoed that but hoped the only arrest warrant the sheriff would have would be for Jewell.

Before the car accident, Jessa had been gunning to add another warrant—for Cooper—for obstruction of justice because she thought he'd tried to stonewall her investigation. He hadn't exactly cooperated, especially with anything that would have brought his father into it, but he darn sure hadn't obstructed anything, either.

As if he could have with the hardheaded Jessa honchoing the investigation.

The car pulled to a stop in the driveway. The windows were heavily tinted, so dark that Cooper couldn't see inside. No one hurried out, but the door to the house opened, and his father stepped onto the porch with them. Cooper had hoped he'd stay inside, but then that wasn't something his father would do. Roy McKinnon wasn't the sort to avoid trouble.

And *trouble* opened both backseat car doors.

A woman stepped out, the spitting image of Jewell. Or at least the Jewell whom Cooper remembered from over two decades ago. Shoulder-length blond hair, slender, almost frail build. In fact, she actually looked frail, something Jewell never had.

"Hello," she said, looking up at them. And she had to look up, all right, because there were twelve steps leading up to the porch. Something Cooper and his brothers had joked about often. But jokes aside, it gave them the catbird seat of sorts, and it put some much needed distance between Jewell and them that Cooper had no intention of narrowing.

"I'm Rosalie," the woman added, her voice as frail as the rest of her.

Rosalie, one of Jewell's twin girls, and his sister. Biologically, anyway. He hadn't seen her since she was barely six years old, but Cooper felt an instant connection with this woman that he darn sure didn't want to feel. He knew from background checks that Rosalie had given birth to a little girl about six months earlier, and the child had been kidnapped from the hospital nursery.

Never to be seen again.

Yeah, there was a connection, all right, and Jessa's hurt little boy had only made that wound fresher for Cooper.

Rosalie stayed by the car and looked over the top to the other side of the vehicle when her fraternal twin got out.

Rayanne.

Nowhere near frail looking.

She had a sturdy build, and her mop of brown hair was gathered into a ponytail. For the most part. Strands of it flew in the steamy August breeze.

Rayanne was wearing jeans, not the designer kind, either, and she had a silver star badge clipped to her leather shoulder holster. She'd been a deputy in a small town two counties over for going on five years now. Her experience showed on her face.

And in that snarl.

That was a McKinnon snarl, one that Cooper recognized because he'd seen it too often in the mirror.

Why the heck did she have to look so much like, well, family?

"Pleased to meet you, too," Rayanne said with a hefty dose of sarcasm in her voice. She turned her eyes on Roy. "Daddy," she said with even more sarcasm and a chip on her shoulder that was bigger than the Smith & Wesson she was toting. Maybe because she blamed Roy for all of this.

Well, the blame was in the car, not with his dad.

"Oh, she'll be fun," Arlene mumbled, mimicking Rayanne's sarcasm.

The driver's-side door opened. Still no Jewell. But it was trouble of a different kind.

FBI agent Seth Calder.

Black hair, black suit and slick black mirrored shades covering his eyes, he stepped out, his phone anchored between his shoulder and his ear. He had that arrogance of a fed written all over him.

Cooper hated him on sight.

The breeze caught the side of his jacket, whipping it back, and the sun hit his holster and badge just right so it glinted in Cooper's eyes. Cooper had to blink and look away for a second.

If his stepbrother even spared them a glance, Cooper couldn't tell. Of course, it was hard to tell much of anything with those sunglasses hiding his eyes.

"Oh, my," Arlene said under her breath. "He looks like something that just stepped out of my dreams."

Cooper and Tucker shot her a glare. "What kind of dreams?" Cooper snarled.

Arlene lifted a graying eyebrow that'd looked

as if it'd never been near tweezers. "The sort you don't want to know I have."

Normally, Cooper would have appreciated the woman's attempt to lighten things up, but there was nothing normal about this.

Still not acknowledging them, Special Agent Calder went to the passenger-side door and opened it. How gentlemanly of him.

Jewell finally made an appearance.

Unlike her stepson, her attention did go straight to them, and a weak smile bent her mouth before it faded in a flash.

She'd changed more than Cooper had thought she would. She still had the blond hair, no grays, and there weren't a lot of wrinkles. She'd been well kept over these years, but her eyes looked old. Maybe because she'd lived with killing a man and abandoning her family all this time. He wanted to think she'd suffered for that, anyway.

"Cooper," she said, her voice small. Her gaze slid to his brothers, and she whispered their names before she settled on Roy. "I know you don't want us here, but the ranch is theirs, too."

"Not his," Tucker said tipping his head to Mr. FBI.

"Seth, too. I adopted him."

"She's my mother," Seth verified, none too friendly like, and he finally put his phone away. He looped his arm around Jewell's waist. "And just so we get this straight, we're here to clear her name."

"Even if it means sullying yours," Rayanne added, and her gaze went right to Roy. Her father. But clearly she didn't think of him that way. Probably because she'd been raised by Jewell's second husband.

"We'll see about that," Cooper fired back at them, and that probably would have started a big family ruckus if Roy hadn't stepped in front of them and if Rosalie hadn't stepped in front of her lot.

It was obvious who the peacemakers were.

And weren't.

Cooper gladly put himself in the second category. He didn't want peace with Jewell or the kids she'd chosen to raise.

"Why don't you show them to the guesthouse, Arlene," Roy suggested.

"Not me." Rayanne grabbed a beat-up gym bag from the car. "I'm not a guest." She marched up the steps as if she had a right to do just that, her gaze locking with Cooper's. The glare she gave him was really a dare, challenging him to stop her from going inside.

"Rayanne, there's plenty of room in the guesthouse," her sister reminded her.

Rayanne didn't take her eyes off Cooper. "I'm a McKinnon, just like you. And besides, there are only two bedrooms in the guesthouse, and I prefer not to have to share a room with my sister. I don't *lay* well with others."

Cooper didn't doubt that one bit and was about to point to the guesthouse anyway, but his father stepped to the side. "There are plenty of rooms upstairs, including yours and Rosalie's." Roy looked at Rosalie then. "You're welcome to join her."

"No, thank you." Rosalie scowled at her sister. "I'm sure everyone would be more comfortable if Seth, Rayanne and I were in the guesthouse."

"Didn't come here to make people comfortable, did I?" Rayanne mumbled, and she pushed past Cooper and went inside.

"I'll show the others to the guesthouse now," Arlene insisted.

It wasn't far, just about twenty yards from the main house, and Jewell no doubt knew the way since her own daddy had built it. However, Arlene's offer was a good one because this family gathering needed to end now.

And not just because Cooper was ready for it to end.

He saw the other car approaching, and even though he didn't recognize the vehicle at first, he recognized the driver when she braked to a noisy stop and threw open the car door.

Jessa.

And she didn't look happy.

Great, she'd found out about the DNA test and would want answers.

"Are you here to take me in?" Jewell immediately asked her.

"No." In fact, Jessa did a sort of double take as if surprised to see Jewell and her entourage there. And maybe she was truly surprised. Because her focus zoomed straight to Cooper.

"We have to talk," Jessa said, and it didn't sound like an invitation, more like an order.

Arlene went down the steps to show the others to the guesthouse just as Jessa stormed up them. His father and brothers gave him a questioning look, but Cooper couldn't explain things yet.

Because he didn't know what to explain.

"This way," Cooper said.

He didn't take Jessa through the main entry but to the side porch so they could go into his home office. It wouldn't exactly be private if Jessa raised her voice.

Something she might very well do.

But his father and brothers were no doubt wrapped up in dealing with Jewell's arrival. Once he'd dealt with this fire, Cooper had to make sure his dad was as okay as he could be under the circumstances.

"Why?" Jessa demanded the moment she stepped inside his office.

Since that *why* could cover a lot of territory, he just waited for her to finish. Cooper reached behind her and shut the door, and his arm accidentally brushed against hers. She jumped as if he'd scalded her.

"You had my son's DNA tested," she went on. But that was as far as she got. Her chest started pumping as if starved for air, and she dropped back and let the now closed door support her.

Jessa wasn't quite as frantic as she had been two days ago at the hospital, but it was darn close. The tiny nicks were still there on her face from her encounter with the air bag, but no business suit today. She was in pants and a sleeveless white top, and she had her hair pulled back in a ponytail. The dark circles under her eyes let him know she hadn't been sleeping.

Neither had he.

It'd taken every ounce of willpower for him not to rush back to the hospital to get a better look at the little boy.

"How's Liam?" he asked. Not avoiding her question. Nothing could do that. He was just delaying it because he truly wanted to know how the toddler was doing.

She glared at him for so long that Cooper wasn't sure she'd answer. "He's better, but you already know that. You've called at least a dozen times checking on his condition."

He had. Cooper also knew Liam was doing so well that he'd probably be released from the hospital tomorrow. Jessa's mom had flown in from Dallas so she could stay with him during his recovery and help Jessa out. Her mom was no doubt with Liam now, since to the best of his knowledge, this was the first time in two days that Jessa had left the hospital.

"He'll make a full recovery?" Cooper asked.

Again, she glared. "Yes. In fact, he already wants to get up and run around. Now, why?" she added without pausing.

Cooper pulled in a long breath that he would need and sank down on the edge of his desk. "Because of the blood-type match. And because we never found my son's body."

Even though she'd no doubt already come up with that answer, Jessa huffed and threw her hands in the air. "And what? You think I found him on the riverbank and pretended to adopt him? Well, I didn't, and Liam's not your son. I want you to put a stop to that DNA test."

Cooper shook his head. "If you're sure he's not my son, then the test will come back as no match."

Her glare got worse. "You're doing this to get back at me." Her breath broke, and the tears came.

Oh, man.

He didn't want this. Not with both of them already emotional wrecks. They were both powder kegs right now, and the flames were shooting all around them. Still, he went closer, and because all those emotions had apparently made him dumber than dirt, Cooper slipped his arm around her.

She fought him. Of course. Jessa clearly didn't want his comfort, sympathy or anything else other than an assurance to put a stop to that test. Still, he held on despite her fists pushing against his chest. One more ragged sob, however, and she sagged against him.

There it was again. That tug deep down in his body. Yeah, dumber than dirt, all right. His body just didn't seem to understand that an attractive woman in his arms could mean nothing.

Even when Jessa looked up at him.

That tug tugged a little harder. Because, yeah, she was attractive, and if the investigation and accusations hadn't cropped up, he might have considered asking her out.

So much for that plan.

"I hate being like this," she said in a breathy whisper. "Hate that all of this is happening." Jessa eased back, looked up at him. "Please tell me you're not doing this because you hate me."

"I'm not doing this because I hate you." And since they were both wearing their hearts on their sleeves, Cooper went a step further. "I don't even hate you. I just don't like what you're trying to do to me and my family."

"It's my job. It's not personal. But this situation with Liam feels personal."

"It *is* personal. I lost my son, and there's a small chance that he's still alive."

Just saying that was too much, and it was Cooper who moved away from her. He wouldn't let her or anyone else see how close this was to breaking him, but it'd brought back all the old memories and gouged into wounds, making them bleed and fester all over again.

"How old was Liam when you adopted him?" Cooper asked.

"Three months old, but that doesn't matter," she quickly added. "I checked, and Liam was born four days after your son."

"Birth records can be altered."

That did it. Jessa the A.D.A. was back. Her chin came up, and even though there were still tears in her eyes, she managed to look tough as nails.

She wasn't.

Cooper was betting she was on the verge of falling apart. Especially if what he was about to show her made the connection that he hoped it'd make.

He took the silver framed photo from his desk.

A photo he looked at every single day, wishing that his life hadn't turned on a dime. Cooper didn't need to look at it now. He'd memorized every detail. It was a picture of Molly sitting in one of the rocking chairs on the front porch. She was holding a tiny Cameron in her arms. The sunlight on their faces.

Keeping his attention pinned to Jessa, he handed her the photo, and after giving him a glance, she studied it.

There.

He saw it in her eyes. That flash of surprise. Maybe even recognition. Because the baby in the picture was only two months younger than Liam was when Jessa adopted him. If Liam was his son, then there'd be a resemblance.

"All babies look the same," she said. But the color had drained from her face.

Cooper figured his color was gone, too, and for a moment he thought he might disgrace himself by dropping to his knees.

His baby was alive.

Well, maybe.

He couldn't jump off that ledge just yet, even though he'd felt more hope than he had in nearly two years. What he needed now were the results of that test, and he reached for his phone to call the doctor again.

However, Jessa's phone buzzed first.

Without taking her gaze off the photo, she blindly groped in her pocket and pulled out her cell. One glance at the screen, however, and she practically tossed the photo back at him so she could hit the answer button.

"Mom, is everything okay?" Jessa quickly asked.

"No," he heard the woman say.

Cooper's heartbeat doubled, and he reached over and moved Jessa back a bit so he could hit the speaker button on her screen.

"What's wrong?" Jessa's voice was trembling now, and she was already opening the door.

"Jessa, you need to get here right away," her mother insisted. "And bring Sheriff McKinnon with you. Someone's trying to kidnap Liam."

Chapter Four

"Why isn't my mother answering her phone?" Jessa snapped, and she tried again. But like the other dozen times, the call went straight to voice mail.

"There are plenty of dead zones in the hospital," Cooper told her. "And maybe your mother turned off the ringer because she's hiding."

It sickened her to think of her mother running through the hospital, trying to protect Liam while kidnappers chased after them.

"Hurry," Jessa said, but she knew Cooper couldn't drive any faster without risking an accident. Still, she wouldn't care if they wrecked as long as she could just see her son.

And prevent him from being kidnapped.

Everything inside her was racing. Her heart. Her breath. The horrible thoughts firing through her head.

The loud wail of the siren didn't help her nerves, but she was thankful for them. Because of the siren and the flashing blue lights, other drivers were moving out of Cooper's way, shaving off precious seconds. Maybe that would be enough.

It *had* to be enough.

She couldn't muffle the sob that tore through her throat. Why was this happening? Why had everything in her life turned upside down?

Another sound shot through the truck, and because her nerves were so frayed, it took her a moment to realize it was Cooper's phone. She didn't see the screen before he sandwiched the phone between his shoulder and his ear.

"It's Reed," he told her.

Reed Caldwell, one of his deputies, and it wasn't Reed's first call but rather his third since this nightmare had begun. Cooper's brothers had called him, also. Tucker and Colt were headed to the hospital in another vehicle.

"No. Stay back," Cooper said to the deputy. "If possible, get me a photo. I'll be there in about five minutes."

That might be five minutes too late.

"Reed's on the scene," Cooper relayed to her the moment he ended the call. "And he just got an update from the security guard. There are two masked men in the hall of the pediatric ward. They're armed, and they've taken a hostage."

Jessa pressed her fists to the sides of her head. "Please, not Liam or my mother."

"No. Not them," Cooper quickly assured her. "They grabbed a nurse when she tried to stop them from entering Liam's room. She screamed, alerted the security guard, and that's when the men put a gun to her head. The security guard wisely backed off and called Reed."

"But what about Liam and my mother?"

"Reed talked to your mother right after she called us. She phoned the 9-1-1 dispatcher, too, and he got her number from them. Reed told her to take Liam into the bathroom of his room and lock the door."

That was a start, but it wasn't nearly enough. Not for her son, her mother or the poor nurse who'd tried to protect Liam.

"There's probably no reception in the bathroom," Cooper went on. "The walls are concrete block."

Jessa prayed that was the only reason her mother wasn't answering the calls. Her mother was a strong, levelheaded person, but an ordeal like this could cause anyone to panic.

"What do these men want?" she asked. "Why did they try to take Liam?"

Cooper shook his head, and for a split second his gaze met hers. She saw the same fear mirrored in his iron-gray eyes that was no doubt in hers. "They've yelled out that they want to talk to you."

Her heart slammed against her chest. So they knew who she was.

Jessa had held out hope that this was some kind of misunderstanding—maybe a situation of mistaken identity or some kind of custody dispute. But if these men had tried to kidnap Liam and then demanded to talk to her, then the chances of a misunderstanding were slim.

"This could be connected to one of your cases," Cooper added. He jammed even harder on the accelerator to pass a car. "Once Liam's safe and these idiots are behind bars, I'll find out."

His jaw muscles were tight again, as were most of the muscles in his body. He seemed absolutely determined to help her son. And she prayed it wasn't because he believed Liam was his. He wasn't Cooper's. He couldn't be.

That was another thing she'd get straight as soon as this was over.

"You told your deputy to stay back," she reminded him. "Why?"

He took the final turn to the hospital. "I don't want to give them a reason to start shooting. Once all the deputies are in place, I'll try to negotiate with them."

Cooper didn't seem like the negotiating type,

but she was. She'd give the men whatever they wanted as long as they left Liam alone.

Without taking his attention off the road, Cooper made another call. "Colt, as soon as Tucker and you arrive, head to the back entrance of the hospital. If it's not clear, clear it. Then get upstairs. Go in low and quiet. Stay out of sight." He paused, glanced at her. And blew out a long breath. "If you need to shoot, just don't miss," Cooper added.

That sent a new round of fear and panic through her. God, she had to get to her baby.

Cooper's phone dinged just as he pulled into the parking lot, and he glanced down at the screen before he handed his phone to her. "Reed just sent me this photo."

It was a grainy shot, obviously taken from a distance, but Jessa could see the two men wearing dark masks. Both were bulky, both armed, and one was indeed holding a terrified-looking woman in front of him like a human shield. The other one was behind his partner. Out of the direct line of fire.

These were the men who wanted her son, and Jessa wished she could reach through the phone lines and stop them.

"I know they're wearing masks, but look at the body language and the hair," Cooper instructed.

"Could one of those men be the person who side-swiped your car?"

Jessa's shoulders snapped back. "You think these things are connected?" But she immediately realized they could very well be.

Mercy, why hadn't she thought of it earlier? If that accident hadn't been an accident, then she should have figured out she and Liam were in danger.

Jessa had to shake her head. "I don't recognize anything about them, but then I barely got a glimpse of the driver."

Cooper gave a weary sigh and braked to a stop directly in front of the emergency room doors, where there were people and staff hurrying out. Jessa reached for the door handle, but he stopped her.

"Look, I know I stand zero chance of asking you to stay in the truck, so here are the rules," he said. "No matter what happens, you stay behind me. No going nuts and trying to get to Liam. No doing or saying anything unless you've cleared it with me first. I sure as hell don't need to babysit you while I'm trying to save Liam."

That stung. Because she didn't need him babysitting her. But Jessa agreed with Cooper only because she wanted him to hurry so they could get inside.

Cooper drew his gun, and she threw open her

door at the same moment that he did and ran toward the emergency room. It wasn't easy because there were about a dozen panicked people still trying to get out. Cooper and she made it through the crowd and bolted up the stairs to the pediatric unit.

They didn't get far.

Deputy Reed Caldwell was there, stooped behind a wall while he peered into the hall. The moment Reed spotted his boss, he shifted over so that Cooper could take the lead. He did. Cooper took aim at the gunmen.

"My brothers just arrived," Cooper said.

Jessa glanced out into the hall, but she didn't get a good enough look before Cooper gave her a warning glare to get back.

"Tucker and Colt are at the other end of the hall, behind the gunmen," Cooper whispered to her. "I'm Sheriff Cooper McKinnon," he called out. "Let the hostage go, put down your gun and let's talk."

Jessa held her breath, praying they would but figuring it was unlikely they'd comply. The men had taken a huge risk in coming here like this, and that meant they wouldn't want to go away empty-handed.

"You wanna protect the little boy inside that room?" one of the men shouted. "There's only one way to do that. Tell Jessa Wells to step out now, or I start shooting. You've got thirty seconds to decide if it's the kid or her."

COOPER HAD TO catch Jessa again to stop her from bolting toward the gunmen. But she didn't exactly cooperate with his attempt to restrain her. She fought, trying to push him away.

"You heard what they said," she snapped, hysteria in her voice.

"Yeah, and I don't believe them. You shouldn't, either. They're criminals, Jessa, and if you go out there, at best they'll gun you down. If you're not so lucky, they'll start shooting up the place, kidnap Liam and take you both to a secondary crime scene. I'll let you guess what they plan to do with you, but I'm thinking it won't be fun for you or Liam."

That froze her, thank goodness, and the tears spilled down her cheeks before she dropped back. Cooper hadn't thought the tears would bother him that much. After all, he'd seen Jessa crying just two days earlier while Liam was in surgery and again when she challenged him about Liam's paternity. But this was different.

Okay, *he* was different.

Because as long as there was a chance that Liam was his, then it upped the stakes a thousand times over. And Jessa was one of the few people who was as aware of that as Cooper.

"You can't let them take him," she whispered. Her mouth was trembling. The rest of her, too. And her eyes begged Cooper to make this situation right.

"I won't let them," Cooper promised, though he had some doubts about the plan he'd come up with.

"Well?" the man shouted. "What'll it be? Because time's up."

Cooper ignored him. "Call Colt," he whispered to Reed. "Tell them to fire on my count of two. The nurse is a head shorter than the gunmen. That gives them six good inches, and I want both men taken out together. I don't want one of these idiots to get off a shot and hurt their hostage."

Reed nodded, did as he said and then moved just to the side of Cooper so he'd be able to fire if necessary. And it just might be necessary if this plan went south.

Cooper glanced down the hall, past the waiting gunmen. The thirty-second time limit was long since up, and it was showing in their body language. They were getting antsy, and the last thing he needed were itchy trigger fingers in an already volatile situation.

"If you think I'm just going to let you walk out of here with the A.D.A. and her son," Cooper told them, "then you're a special kind of stupid. Put down your guns now!"

That stirred them up. They cursed. Fired nervy glances all around them. Trying to figure out what to do.

Had they really thought he wouldn't challenge them or try to stop them? Maybe they'd heard of the discord between him and Jessa and thought he'd turn a blind eye so they could kidnap her.

He wouldn't do that. Not ever.

Cooper took a deep breath. Readied his gun. And nodded for Reed to do the same.

"On the count of three, put down your guns," Cooper called out to the men. He added a quick silent prayer and shouted, "One."

Cooper checked to see if the men had come to their senses. They hadn't. They were cursing now and dragging their captive toward Liam's door. A door they were no doubt ready to bash open so they could take the little boy.

That wasn't going to happen, either.

"Two!" Cooper shouted.

Everything seemed to happen at once. The gunman darted away from his comrade and reached for the door. In the same motion, he fired a shot at Cooper.

Cooper ducked back, dodging the bullet, but two thick blasts followed. Not from the gunmen. These had come from the other end of the hall, where his brothers were. He looked out, spotted both of them on each side of the corridor. Cooper spotted the gunmen, too.

Both on the floor.

They weren't dead, but they'd been injured and were writhing and groaning. They were loud, but not nearly as loud as the nurse. Screaming, she bolted away from the men and ran right toward him.

"You're okay," Cooper assured her and handed the woman off to Reed. He had to move fast because Jessa started sprinting, headed directly for Liam's room.

She'd have to go past the men to get there.

Cooper caught up with her, pulling her behind him, and he kicked the men's guns away from their hands. The moment he did that, a medic came forward. So did his brothers, and Cooper knew the situation was under control. Jessa, however, wasn't.

"I have to see Liam," she insisted.

"Yeah, I know." Cooper felt the same, and he didn't have the same ties to Liam as Jessa did. She'd raised him. Still, the urgency pressed down on him like a lead weight.

Cooper eased open Liam's door, and with his gun still at the ready, he peered inside. No other gunmen. Thank God. So he continued to the bathroom.

"Mrs. Wells?" Cooper tapped on the jamb. "It's Sheriff McKinnon."

He heard movement, and it wasn't long before Jessa's mom opened the door. She was holding a sleeping Liam in her arms.

"Is he okay?" Jessa didn't wait for her mother to answer. She gently took Liam and pressed a flurry of kisses on his face and head.

"He's fine," her mother answered.

But Cooper couldn't say the same for the woman. She was shaking so hard that she collapsed into Cooper's arms. "It's okay," he assured her. "You're safe now."

But for how long?

Cooper didn't have an answer for that—yet.

"Wait here," he said to the women, and he went back into the hall to see if he could get some quick answers. Apparently luck wasn't on his side today, because both gunmen were unconscious. And they were both bleeding a lot. It meant no answers now. Maybe not ever if they didn't make it through this. Still, it was better than the alternative of having a dead nurse and Jessa and Liam kidnapped.

"Can you handle this?" Cooper asked, his gaze going first to Colt before swinging to Reed.

Both his deputies nodded.

That was the only assurance Cooper needed. There was a crowd of people now. Medics and doctors who'd responded to treat the wounded men. Some gawkers, too. Cooper picked through the group until his attention landed on Dr. Howland.

"I have to get Liam out of here," Cooper said. "He'll need a car seat and his meds."

The doctor didn't argue. "We can use my assistant's car. It has an infant seat already in it. I'll get her keys and my bag so I can go with you."

Cooper didn't argue, either. Despite Jessa's earlier assurances that Liam was making a speedy recovery, Cooper figured he'd need medical care for a while.

It didn't take long for the doc to return, and Cooper went back into the room. He pulled the blanket from Liam's crib and draped it over the toddler.

"Come with me," Cooper told the women. He positioned himself in front of them as they made their way into the hall.

The wounded gunmen were gone, no doubt on their way to surgery, but there were large pools of blood on the floor.

"Follow us out," Cooper said to his brother Tucker. It wouldn't hurt to have some extra firepower if things turned bad again.

With Tucker behind them, Cooper led Jessa and her mother around the blood as best he could, and they followed Dr. Howland down the corridor.

"Where are we going?" Jessa asked. She was holding Liam as if he were a thin piece of glass ready to shatter.

Cooper glanced around to make sure no one was in hearing range. There wasn't anyone. They had the hall to themselves.

"We're going somewhere you aren't going to like," he mumbled.

Cooper was taking Liam, Jessa and her mother home with him.

Chapter Five

Nothing about this felt right.

Jessa stared down at her sleeping son, thankful that none of this seemed to be affecting him.

But it was certainly affecting her.

The spent adrenaline had left her bone tired, but despite that she hadn't slept more than a few minutes in the guest room at the McKinnon ranch. Her mind was still wired, and the thoughts of how wrong this was kept going through her head.

Along with the sound of those shots.

She would always hear those. Would always remember how close they'd come to her baby.

And she would never forget that Cooper and his brothers had been the ones to keep Liam safe. Of course, Cooper might have had an ulterior motive for what he'd done.

Because he might believe Liam was his son.

Just the thought of that revved up her heartbeat and caused her breath to go thin. Jessa tried to tamp down her emotions. No need to worry about what might be, and she refused to believe that Liam was Cooper's lost child. Her life and luck couldn't take another bad turn like that, and she had to be due for the peaceful life that she'd planned with her son.

Of course, Cooper might be making the same plans.

Jessa glanced at the laptop still open on the guest bed where she had tried to sleep. She'd closed the email containing the background check on Cooper that she'd asked a P.I. friend to do, but she didn't need to see the report to remember what it'd said.

From all accounts, Cooper had been crazy in love with his wife, Molly, but they'd gotten off to a rocky start. Molly had literally broken her engagement to another man to start seeing Cooper, and the other man—Donovan Bradley—had then in turn tried to have embezzlement charges filed against Molly for the cattle-broker business they'd run together. The charges hadn't stuck.

But the gossip had.

There were plenty of rumors that Cooper had slept with Donovan's fiancée just to get back at the man for an old feud between the former friends turned enemies. Jessa had seen photos of Cooper and Donovan together on the high school football team and again on the rodeo circuit—definitely friends in those days—but something had caused a rift. Rumor had it that Donovan had gotten too friendly with Cooper's aunt, who was close to their age. Another side believed that Cooper was at fault with his sexual pursuit of Molly.

Jessa wanted to believe the rumors. She wanted to believe anything that would help her discredit Cooper, but she hadn't found a shred of proof that he was anything but a badge-wearing cowboy who actually knew the meaning of justice.

And keeping his jeans zipped.

Unlike Donovan, he hadn't left a string of broken hearts throughout the county.

Jessa's phone vibrated, and she silently groaned at the name she saw on the screen. It was yet another badge-wearing cowboy.

County Sheriff Aiden Braddock.

Aiden's father, Whitt, was the man Jewell was charged with murdering.

Jessa had worked closely with Aiden to bring the charges against Cooper's mother. For months the investigation had consumed them. Now she had something else more important to consume her—keeping her son safe and making other arrangements that didn't involve staying on the McKinnon ranch.

Jessa stepped out in the hall to take the call so that she wouldn't wake Liam, and she nearly ran right into Cooper. He'd obviously just showered.

His hair was still damp, and he smelled, well, better than he should have. Something musky and manly that seemed to alert every nerve in her body. Ditto for his cowboy-cop "uniform" of worn jeans, a pale blue button-up shirt and scuffed cowboy boots. His badge was clipped to his belt.

Next to the silver rodeo buckle.

If she'd had any doubts that he was a cowboy, that would have rid her of them.

"That'll be Sheriff Braddock," he said, tipping his head to her still-vibrating phone. Mercy. The sight of Cooper had made her forget all about it. "He just called to tell me that Jewell turned herself in to the county deputy and she's now under arrest."

Since it wasn't a conversation she wanted to have in front of Cooper, she let the call go to voice mail. Better to get any details later after she'd worked out some details and rules of her own.

"I didn't tell Sheriff Braddock or anyone else that you were here," Cooper added.

Good. For now, the fewer people who knew where she was, the better. "Any updates on the would-be kidnappers?"

"One didn't make it. The other came through surgery all right but is still too weak to talk. Colt's posted outside the guy's door in case someone tries to help him escape. Colt will call to let me know when I can question him."

Jessa hated those men, but she wished both were alive and ready to spill why they'd tried to take her baby.

Cooper glanced down at her clothes as if he'd never before seen jeans on a woman. And he hadn't on her. She always tried to dress the part of the D.A. when she went out, even just to get groceries. Yes, it might seem silly, but she wanted to be set apart, wanted the locals to respect her for the job.

But the jeans clearly didn't get much respect from Cooper.

However, they did garner a long look. One that made her feel as if he was trying to undress her.

Cooper glanced over her shoulder, his attention landing on the crib. "Is Liam okay?"

But he didn't just ask the question. Cooper slid past her, his arm brushing against hers, and went into the room. He stayed back from the crib, but he could no doubt see her baby's face. Yes, it was petty, but she stepped between them. However, since he was taller than she was, he'd have no trouble getting a second look.

"He's fine," she snapped, her voice still a whisper. "The doctor examined him before he left last night, and your sister came by a half hour ago to check his bandage. She said he was fine, and then she and my mother went to the kitchen to get something to eat."

His sister Rosalie, who was a pediatric nurse. For Liam's sake, it was convenient that she was at the ranch with them, but her mere presence was another sticking point. Because the only reason Rosalie was there was to help clear her mother's name. That put Jessa and her at odds.

In theory, anyway.

But Rosalie hadn't shown any resentment whatsoever. She'd examined Liam as if he were her own child and had promised to check on him as long as needed.

Hopefully, that wouldn't be long.

Jessa motioned for them to go back out in the hall. She didn't want Cooper standing there staring at Liam. Especially staring at him with that hopeful, pained look in his eyes.

Cooper followed her. Finally.

"I'll need to make arrangements to leave," she started. But that was as far as she got.

"Not yet. I want you, your mom and Liam here until I have a handle on who's after Liam and why."

Jessa groaned. "That could take days or more."

"Or less," he quickly argued. "We'll start with the gunmen, and once we know who they are, then we can work backward to find out who hired them." He paused a second. "Any idea who that would have been and why?"

She shook her head. "Maybe it's someone connected to your mother."

A muscle flickered in his jaw.

"I'm not accusing you," Jessa explained. "But there are others involved in the murder investigation."

"My brothers. My dad. And my mother's three other kids. Yeah, I know what you think of us. I can personally vouch for my brothers and Dad. Rosalie, too," he added almost hesitantly. "The other two, Rayanne and Seth, are law enforcement officers."

It wasn't exactly an endorsement of the last two's innocence, but there was another player in this.

Jewell.

"Do you think your mother murdered Whitt Braddock?" Jessa came out and asked.

"I don't care if she did."

Yes, he did. The wounds were still there. After all, his mother had abandoned him and his brothers. Jessa couldn't imagine doing that to Liam, but then she also couldn't imagine being a married woman, having an affair and then killing her lover.

But that was exactly what Jewell had done.

Well, it was what the evidence pointed to her doing, anyway.

"When I was at the hospital giving blood," Cooper continued, "you said you'd made some inquiries about Liam's birth parents, so that you'd know the family's medical history. Who exactly did you contact?"

She blinked and had to think hard to remember that conversation. "My adoption attorney, Hector Dixon. Why, you don't think he had anything to do with this, do you?"

Cooper lifted his shoulder. "I need to look at all possible angles. Maybe Hector contacted someone who got spooked."

Even though he hadn't come out and said it, Jessa knew where this was going. "You think the adoption was illegal—"

"Again, I'm looking at all angles. How'd Hector react when you asked him about the birth parents?"

Jessa opened her mouth to assure him that Hector had reacted as expected. But he hadn't. "He seemed nervous. Maybe distracted," she corrected. "He's a busy man, and I called him out of the blue. He might have thought I was questioning the way he handled the adoption."

At least she hoped that was all there was to it.

"I'll get him to the sheriff's office and question him," Cooper insisted.

Again, she nearly jumped to assure him that it wouldn't be necessary, that she'd talk to her lawyer herself. But this was an official investigation now. Besides, Hector might have some idea why this had happened, and if he did, he might know something that would somehow keep Liam safe.

"What about your personal relationships?" Cooper asked. "Maybe your ex wanted to make trouble for you?"

Jessa felt the heat rise in her cheeks. Cooper knew. Of course he did. He had access to police records from all over the state. He would have seen the report that she'd filed when her ex-husband, Rick Bolton, had beaten her. Maybe Cooper had even seen the bloody and bruised photos taken of her so he could be arrested for assault and battery.

"My ex hasn't been in touch with me for nearly three years," she settled for saying. "I'm not even sure where he is."

She braced herself for Cooper's argument. That Rick could have decided to get even with her for the eight months he'd spent in jail. But no argument—Cooper's eyes met hers for just a moment before they darted away. In that second of time, she thought maybe she'd seen some sympathy.

But she had to be wrong about that.

He was still too enraged about her bringing

Jewell back to Sweetwater Springs and therefore back into his life.

"Where'd your lawyer get Liam?" Cooper asked.

They were back to the illegal adoption theory, and while it was a definite sore point, it was something she, too, wanted to know. It wouldn't help if she just buried her head in the sand.

"It was a private adoption, but let me call Hector now and find out."

She stepped away from Cooper before she could hear any reason he might have for her not doing that. But he didn't object. Instead, when she took her phone from her pocket and pressed Hector's number, Cooper just stayed in the doorway, looking at Liam.

"He's not yours," Jessa insisted. "If he were, I'd know it. I'd feel it in my heart."

It was a stupid argument. One that clearly didn't convince Cooper. He just made one of those annoying sounds that could have meant anything. Jessa didn't get a chance to continue the one-sided disagreement, because Hector answered.

"Jessa," he greeted. "I heard about your car accident. Are Liam and you all right?"

It seemed the right thing to ask, but Jessa's nerves were too close to the surface for her to take anything at face value. "We're fine, but that's not why I'm calling. I need to know what you learned about Liam's birth parents."

"Nothing," Hector readily admitted. "Look, I've been trying, but the birth mother was adamant about this being a closed adoption. She left no contact information whatsoever."

That wasn't unusual. Often a teen mother would close that door of contact as her way of moving on and detaching herself from the child.

"What adoption agency did you use?" Jessa pressed.

Hector hesitated. It wasn't a pause. Jessa could feel the difference, but she prayed she was wrong. She didn't want any hesitations when he came to this.

"No agency," Hector finally said. "The woman I used is more or less a broker, and she's got a good reputation for her placements."

Jessa was listening to every word, but she lost her focus when Cooper went into the room with Liam. She went after him.

"Birth mothers who want to do private adoptions contact this broker," Hector continued, "and she in turn contacts the attorneys of prospective birth parents who are willing to pay medical bills and maybe even give compensation. Like you did."

She had. A total payment of nearly fifty thousand dollars, which was almost every bit of the inheritance she'd gotten when her father died six years earlier. Jessa would have paid a heck of a lot more than that. But again, that wasn't what had her attention now. Cooper had it. And she found him right by the crib, staring down at Liam.

Then she saw something else.

Cooper smiled.

The corner of his mouth lifted, the simple gesture flickering the muscle in his jaw. It was short-lived when his gaze landed on the bandage across Liam's stomach. The incision beneath it was already healing, but the bandage was a reminder that she'd come close to losing him.

"Jessa?" Hector said. "Did you hear me?"

No. She hadn't. "I'm sorry, this is a bad connection," Jessa lied.

"I said in our case, the broker contacted me because she'd heard through mutual friends that you wanted to adopt a newborn."

It all sounded reasonable. So reasonable that it might even appease Cooper.

"What's the broker's name?" Jessa asked. Best to finish this conversation fast so she could maneuver Cooper out of the room and away from Liam.

But Hector didn't do much to finish things. His hesitation lasted a lot longer than the first one. "Her name is Peggy Dawes, but please don't contact her. She prefers not to deal directly with the adoptive parents."

Tough. This broker would deal with her. "I need her phone number. Before you say no, it's important. Yesterday someone tried to kidnap my baby, and I want to know why."

"Good God. And you think Peggy has answers about that?" He didn't wait for her to respond. "She won't. Heavens, Jessa. How could you think that? Peggy did you a great service by locating a baby for you, and you can't go around questioning—"

"I'll thank her," Jessa interrupted. "Now give me her phone number."

The seconds crawled by before she heard some rustling on the other end of the line and then Hector rattled off the number. Jessa made a note of it on her phone's notepad.

"Thanks," Jessa mumbled.

"Don't thank me. I'll keep looking for info on Liam's birth parents, but I'm not doing you any favors by giving you Peggy's number."

Jessa froze. "What do you mean?" But she was talking to the air because Hector had already hung up.

"Anything wrong?" Cooper asked.

He'd no doubt seen the concern on her face, but Jessa shook her head and showed him the number she'd taken down. "It's for Peggy Dawes, the baby broker my attorney used. Hector is still looking for information about Liam's birth parents."

Cooper nodded and pressed in Peggy's numbers on his phone's keypad.

"No!" Jessa insisted. "I don't want you to call her. I'll do it. I don't want her to think she's under investigation or something."

"She *is* under investigation," Cooper fired back, and he would have pressed the call button if Jessa hadn't caught his hand to stop him.

Jessa was about to launch into another argument, but the sound stopped both of them. Not a gunshot or some other nightmarish noise.

Liam stirred. "Mama." And he reached for her.

That got her hand off Cooper, and she shoved her phone into her pocket so she could gently lift Liam into her arms. He showed no signs whatsoever of being in pain, though he did point to his bandage. "Got boo-boo."

And then his attention went to Cooper.

Liam eyed him as if sizing him up, but then his attention landed on the shiny badge and rodeo buckle. "Up." Liam reached out for Cooper to take him.

It felt as if someone had punched her. Jessa didn't want her baby in the arms of the man who might try to take him away from her.

But that was exactly what Cooper did.

He eased his hands around Liam and lifted him into his arms. Liam didn't try to inspect the shiny things that had caused him to reach for Cooper. Her son just studied him.

Then Liam smiled.

Cooper closed his eyes a moment, and she could almost see the painful memories tightening the muscles in his face. Heaven knew how much he'd grieved when he'd lost his son in that flood. Jessa suddenly knew how painful that would have been, because she was feeling a little of it now.

God, she couldn't lose him. *Wouldn't.* Because she refused to believe Cooper had any kind of claim on the child she loved more than life itself.

Cooper's phone buzzed, and he hesitated as if deciding whether to answer it. He had no choice, of course, because it could be about the investigation, but it meant handing Liam back to her so he could answer it.

"It's Colt," he relayed to her, and he stepped away from the crib to take the call. He didn't put it on speaker, and Jessa couldn't hear what Colt was saying, but she prayed it wasn't more bad news.

She watched, waited and kept Liam close.

"Yeah, I heard you," Cooper said to his brother. "No, I'll handle it. I'll talk to her."

Mercy, that didn't sound good.

"We have IDs on the gunmen," Cooper explained the moment he ended the call.

Jessa was afraid to feel any real relief, but that was a start. Cooper had already said if he had names, he could begin to look for connections.

"The surviving one is Vernon Graham," Cooper went on. "He's awake and says he wants you to offer him a plea deal for a lighter sentence."

"What will he give us in return?" Jessa asked, and she was almost afraid to hear the answer. So far, nothing about this situation was good.

Cooper paused a heartbeat, his gaze fastening to hers. "Graham says he'll tell us the name of the person who hired him to kidnap Liam."

Chapter Six

"You don't have to do this," Cooper reminded Jessa one more time. "In fact, I'd rather you didn't."

She shot him a glare, kept her arms folded over her chest and continued to stare out his truck window at the passing countryside. "I want to hear what this woman has to say," Jessa mumbled.

This woman was Peggy Dawes.

Vernon Graham had given them Peggy's name as part of a plea deal. Judging from Jessa's scowl and body language, she wasn't pleased about the gunman's revelation that Peggy was the one who'd hired him to kidnap Liam. And there was a good reason for Jessa's anger.

It meant the kidnapping attempt was linked to the adoption. And it also could mean the whole adoption deal had been illegal.

But now Cooper was the one to snarl.

If Liam was indeed his son, then how the heck had Peggy gotten her hands on him?

Unfortunately, he could think of a few scenarios that tightened the knot in his gut. Maybe Peggy or one of her baby-brokering henchmen had caused his wife to be swept away in the flood. Or it could have gone in a different direction and Peggy merely could have found Liam. Of course, that led him to the next question of why she hadn't just called the cops and reported it.

There was also another possible conclusion.

Maybe the gunman had out-and-out lied.

That also didn't help with the knot, because it still meant this was somehow connected to the adoption. After all, how else would the gunman have known the woman's name?

He would soon know the answer to that, since he was headed out to Peggy's San Antonio house to have a little chat with her. Cooper had considered just hauling her into the sheriff's office for questioning, but the woman didn't have even a parking ticket, much less a criminal record. Also, other than the accusations of would-be kidnappers, there were no flags to indicate she was doing anything illegal. Heck, he couldn't even find a connection between her and the gunman, Graham, who'd accused her of wrongdoing.

Well, he couldn't find the connection yet, anyway.

But if either Graham or Peggy confessed to

anything, Cooper would be making an arrest today. That was why he'd wanted his brother along.

Jessa's phone buzzed, and she snatched it up and put it to her ear, but not before Cooper saw that the call was from her mother. "Is something wrong?" Jessa immediately asked the caller.

"No, everything's fine," he heard Linda say.

Thankfully, Jessa and he were close enough that he had no trouble hearing the conversation. He'd taken precautions when Jessa had said she'd be going with him to see Peggy. Cooper had put all the ranch hands on alert, and Tucker was standing guard. Rayanne was also in the house, but he hadn't even bothered to ask her to help. Unlike Rosalie, Rayanne didn't seem to be the helping sort.

Still, there were plenty of things that could go wrong that didn't involve security, so Cooper listened carefully to what Linda had to say.

"I just wanted you to know that Dr. Howland was here to check on Liam, and he said he was doing great," Linda explained. "He didn't feel there was any need to move him back to the hospital as long as Rosalie continues to change and check the bandage."

Jessa huffed softly. And Cooper knew why. It meant she'd have to stay at the ranch. Of course, she could just hire another nurse and leave, and Cooper figured Jessa was already working on that.

He was working on making her stay.

Until the DNA results came back, Cooper wanted Liam under the McKinnon roof. And after he had the results… Well, he'd deal with that when and if the time came.

"Thanks, Mom," Jessa said. "Give Liam a kiss for me."

Jessa put her phone away and continued to look out the window. Cooper did his own share of looking, too. First to make sure they weren't being followed by anyone but Colt, who was driving behind them in his truck.

But Cooper also looked at Jessa.

No matter how many times he told his eyes to stay off her, they didn't listen. Partly because of the worry and fear still on her face. Partly because he shared the same concern about Liam's safety as she did.

However, it was her jeans and snug red top that were giving him the most trouble.

There was nothing particularly special about the items of clothing, except they looked damn good on her. Hugging her curves. Making him well aware that beneath her A.D.A. facade, there was a red-blooded woman.

One who stirred his own blood.

And that couldn't happen.

Hell.

He wasn't in any position to start a relationship, especially with a woman who thought he was lower than grit on a horse's hoof. And besides, he had to focus on getting things straight with this adoption and the attack. It wasn't as if he didn't have enough to keep him busy.

"You keep looking at me," she grumbled.

Yeah, he did. "It's nothing personal," Cooper said, and then silently cursed. Obviously, her jeans had also rendered him stupid.

Because a man gawking at a woman was indeed personal.

"I meant it doesn't mean anything," he corrected. "It's just you look, well, different. Sort of naked without one of your suits."

What he should have done was just shut the heck up instead of babbling like an idiot.

Her eyebrow slid up. "Naked?"

He groaned. Best to go another round of trying to clear this up. "Normal. Like you fit in around here."

She looked at him as if he'd sprouted an extra nose or something. Obviously, he'd missed the mark.

"If I fit in, I won't get the respect I need," she said, her voice crisp. The clothes might be different, but that ice-queen voice was the same. "I'd be just one of the good ol' boys."

"No one would ever suspect you of being a boy," he grumbled.

However, it was interesting that Jessa thought she had to keep her outsider status to do her job. He might not like the accusations she'd made against him, but he'd never wanted her to feel that she had to build up walls to stay professional.

She stared at him, whispered something he didn't catch and looked away. "Whatever this feeling is between us, it can't mean anything."

That sounded pretty good, but then she gave him one last glance. Or rather she gave that glance to his jeans.

Oh, man.

One-sided personal was bad enough, but two-sided could get them in a mess of trouble. Thankfully, he got a reprieve from putting his foot in his mouth because the GPS announced they had arrived at their destination.

The modest redbrick house was in a subdivision in an equally modest part of town. Definitely not the home of a lucrative baby broker. Of course, it could be a front, so as not to draw attention, and that meant they needed to take precautions. If Peggy had been the one to hire those two men, then she might have even more men and guns inside.

Cooper waited until Colt was parked and out of his truck before he motioned for Jessa to exit.

"Yes, I know," Jessa said without his prompting. "I stay behind you, and I don't take any chances."

But she would take chances. To protect Liam, she'd do anything, and that was why he had to watch her as carefully as he watched Peggy. If he'd thought for one minute that Jessa wouldn't have followed him for this visit, he would have just demanded that she stay at the ranch.

They walked to the porch, with Jessa between them, and Cooper rang the bell. There was a camera mounted just above the door and it didn't take long before the woman's voice poured through the little intercom just beneath the camera.

"May I help you?" she asked.

Both Colt and he flashed their badges. "I'm Sheriff Cooper McKinnon. This is Deputy Colt McKinnon and A.D.A. Jessa Wells. We need to talk to you."

The door instantly opened, so fast that Cooper nearly reached for his gun, but the woman he came face-to-face with wasn't armed. She was a tall, attractive blonde in her mid-to late thirties, and there was little chance she could be carrying concealed in the gauzy white summer dress she was wearing. It fit her like a glove.

The woman's attention snapped right to Jessa. "Jessa Wells?" Peggy asked, her breath already revved up. "Did something else happen to the little boy you adopted?"

Well, at least Peggy wasn't going to claim that she knew nothing about the reason for their visit, and she certainly wasn't acting like a woman with anything to hide.

Of course, she could just be a really good liar.

Jessa nodded in response to Peggy's question. "Someone tried to kidnap him yesterday."

"Oh, God." And Peggy just kept repeating it while she motioned for them to come inside.

They went in, Cooper's gaze firing all around to make sure they weren't about to be ambushed. At first he thought he heard someone talking, but he realized it was music. Peggy apparently liked country music and white furniture. In fact, the whole place was pretty sterile looking. Nothing, however, to indicate she was making big bucks with illegal adoptions.

"Sit down, please," Peggy said. "Could I get you a drink or something?" Again, her focus was on Jessa.

"No, thank you. We're just here to find out about the man who attempted to take my son." Jessa glanced at Cooper, silently asking how much she should say. He didn't want all the details spilled about the DNA test, not yet anyway, so he took things from there.

"Two men wearing masks showed up at the

hospital," Cooper explained, and he looked for any sign of guilt or recognition in her eyes. "One was killed. The other is Vernon Graham. He was injured, but he was able to talk today." He paused, kept watching Peggy's face. "And he claims you hired him to kidnap Liam."

Well, he got a reaction, but it wasn't one of guilt. Peggy's breath burst out, and she got to her feet. She pressed her hands against the sides of her head. "This can't be happening. It just can't be."

Cooper stood, positioning himself in front of Jessa just in case Peggy panicked and tried to run. But she didn't appear to be on the verge of doing anything but breaking down into tears.

And yeah, they came.

The tears started to streak down her cheeks. They were sort of convincing for an innocent woman, except guilty people cried crocodile tears all the time.

"You know Vernon Graham?" Cooper asked.

"No, of course not." She leaned forward, catching Jessa's hand. "I really just want to help people. Women like you. I have a large circle of friends, and when I hear of someone who's chosen to given up her baby, then I look for the right family for the child."

"You're a baby broker," Cooper concluded. "You get paid to do what you do."

Peggy's mouth tightened a little. "Yes, I get paid. Not as much as you'd think, and I'm not a broker. I think of myself more as a matchmaker. I find the perfect fit for babies."

"Admirable," he mumbled, and he hoped he didn't sound too sarcastic. It was hard to give the woman an inch of leeway when she'd been named a felony suspect. Of course, she'd been named that by yet another felon. "So why did Graham say you'd hired him to kidnap Liam?"

She instantly shook her head, her blond curls swinging around her face. "I don't know. But something suspicious is going on. I'm almost certain that someone's been following me, and then three days ago, I got a visit from a P.I."

Jessa and he exchanged glances. The timing was certainly suspect because that was the day of Jessa's car accident. Also the day that Cooper had requested a DNA test on Liam. He'd made waves to get the court order for that test, and in doing so, he could have stirred up some trouble from someone who didn't want trouble stirred.

Cooper snagged Peggy's gaze so he could watch her reaction to his question. "What makes you think someone's following you?"

"Just a feeling I keep getting. Like I'm being watched."

Cooper didn't discount it. Gut feelings had saved him more than a time or two, but he didn't like the gut feeling he was getting about Peggy, either.

"What P.I.?" Jessa asked the woman.

More head shaking from Peggy. "I can't remember his name. He only spoke to me for a minute or two. Said he was representing a client who was considering adoption. All he wanted to know was how I handled my paperwork for the adoptions. I told him there was no paperwork, that it was all done by word of mouth. I've been doing this for years, but that's the first time I've had a visit from a P.I."

"And he didn't say anything specifically about Liam?" Jessa pressed.

"No. He didn't ask about any of the babies that I've helped place, and there have been dozens of them." Peggy paused. "Do you think this man was working for the kidnappers?"

"Possibly," Cooper answered. "And that's why we need his name."

"I have his card somewhere around here." She stood and went to a rolltop desk in the corner. When she lifted the top, Cooper saw the stacks of papers and books. Definitely not as sterile and pristine as the rest of the house. Peggy began to dig through the heaps.

He hoped there wasn't a gun hidden in that mess.

Just in case there was, Cooper moved to the

edge of his seat so he could watch Peggy better. "Where'd you get Liam?"

"I didn't *get* him. That's not how it works. I simply put Hector Dixon in touch with this friend of a friend who had the baby. The baby wasn't even her own child. If I remember correctly, she said someone in her family, a teenager, had given birth and couldn't keep the baby."

"I need that friend of a friend's name," Cooper insisted. "Or have you forgotten it, too?"

For just a moment she got a deer-caught-in-headlights look, but then she nodded. Swallowed hard. "What if the person who hired these kidnappers sends someone to come after me?" Peggy asked.

"Why would he?" Cooper pressed, though if the woman was an innocent pawn in all of this, he knew a good reason why. Peggy could be a dangerous loose end for someone trying to cover up an illegal adoption.

"I can arrange for you to have some protection," Cooper offered.

Peggy nodded. Stared at him for a moment and continued to dig through the papers. She finally extracted what appeared to be a bill with something jotted on it.

"It's not the P.I.'s card, but it is the name of the friend of a friend who contacted me about

Liam." Peggy scanned through the notes. "Her name was Carol Sealey."

Jessa shook her head, no doubt because the name meant nothing to her. But it sure as hell meant something to Cooper. Colt, too. He opened his mouth to say something, but Cooper gave him a stay-quiet look.

Hell.

This had just taken a really bad turn.

"I have another desk in my bedroom," Peggy said. "I'll look for the P.I.'s card there."

Cooper didn't tell her to stop, and he didn't go after her. Heck, he wasn't even sure he could move. He just sat there and waited for the woman to scurry out of the room.

"Who's Carol Sealey?" Jessa whispered.

"She works as a personal assistant for Donovan Bradley," Cooper managed to say.

Judging from the way her eyes widened and the hard breath she sucked in, Jessa not only knew who he was. She also knew of Donovan's connection to him.

Of course she did.

There was still a lot of gossip about Donovan and him, and Jessa would have uncovered it when she was investigating him for those unfounded obstruction-of-justice charges.

"Donovan hates Cooper," Colt offered.

"He was once engaged to your late wife," Jessa added. "And then he was involved with Jewell's younger sister. Not in a good way, either. I've heard there was possibly some physical abuse."

Yeah, she knew the whole story, all right. What she didn't know was that in addition to the pain Donovan had inflicted on his aunt, the man had also tried to cause Molly and him as much trouble as possible. Nothing criminal, just the constant flow of malicious rumors and attempts to destroy Molly's reputation and the day care and preschool that she'd worked so hard to get started.

Jessa made a soft gasp, no doubt coming to the conclusion that Cooper and Colt had already reached. If Donovan's lackey, Carol Sealey, had some part in the adoption, then it was likely Donovan had, too.

And that would mean Donovan could have stolen Liam.

But how?

Molly had been swept away in the flood. She'd drowned. Cooper had seen her body, and there'd been no signs of foul play. Nothing to indicate that the baby could have survived, either.

But he could have.

No gasp this time. Jessa huffed, got to her feet. "Don't jump to conclusions."

Too late. Cooper had already made the jump. "I need the results of that DNA test." And he took out his phone.

"Please, no," Jessa whispered.

Cooper looked up at her, bracing himself for her to try to stop him from making the call. But her words seemed to be a prayer. No doubt praying that Liam's DNA didn't match his. But now that Donovan's employee was the one who'd arranged for Liam's adoption, it was the only thing that made sense.

Unless Peggy was lying.

Since Jessa had heard the stories about Donovan, Molly and him, it wasn't much of a stretch that Peggy could have heard them, too.

Cursing, Cooper jumped off the sofa, and drawing his gun, he hurried down the hall where he'd last seen Peggy. There were three rooms off the hall. Two doors were open. The other closed. That was where Cooper headed.

"Peggy?" he called out.

No answer.

Gun first, Cooper stepped into the doorway, his gaze slashing from one side to the other. Movement caught his eye, and he took aim. However, it was only the wind stirring the white curtains in the window that was wide-open.

Peggy was gone.

Chapter Seven

Jessa's mind was running wild, and it was hard to tamp down the bad thoughts when there were so many of them. She hadn't wanted any of the danger to be connected to the adoption, but with every turn, they kept coming back to it. And now someone who could have given them answers was missing.

Where the heck was Peggy?

Jessa couldn't hear the phone conversation that Cooper was having with Tucker, but judging from his body language, the search for Peggy wasn't going well. He was pacing the sunroom that stretched across the back of the McKinnon house. He was barking out orders, too, but so far none of the orders or the search had turned up anything. It was as if the woman had vanished.

"It's amazing how fast babies heal," Rosalie said as she changed Liam's bandage. She finished up, gave him a kiss on the cheek and stood from the wicker chair where she'd been seated.

Jessa thanked her, something she'd been doing a lot lately. She thanked her mother, too, and glanced at Liam to make sure he was okay. He was. He was totally engrossed in the book Linda was reading to him.

"I can watch Liam," Rosalie offered, "if you and your mom want to take a nap. You both look exhausted."

Jessa didn't doubt what Rosalie was saying, but a nap was out of the question for her. No way would she be able to let her body and mind rest with so much up in the air.

"I can't lose him," Jessa mumbled. She hadn't meant to blurt that out, but she was doing it a lot lately.

Rosalie nodded, and she gave Jessa's arm a pat. It was more than just sympathy coming from the woman. From what Jessa had heard, Rosalie's newborn daughter had been kidnapped, never to be seen again. Rosalie knew what it was like to lose a child. Cooper did, too.

And it was something Jessa never wanted to experience.

"I've been investigating missing children," Rosalie said. "I've made plenty of contacts. I could ask around and see if anyone knows something about the circumstances surrounding Liam's adoption."

"There's nothing to find," Jessa insisted. *I*

hope. "But if you hear anything that'll lead us to the kidnapper, that would help."

Rosalie nodded, assured her that she would do just that and walked away.

Cooper finished his call and looked on the verge of cursing a blue streak before his attention landed on Liam. That softened his expression a bit.

"No sign of Peggy, and no one's been able to reach Donovan Bradley," he explained, shaking his head. "Carol Sealey no longer works for Donovan. His new assistant said she has no idea where Carol is and that Donovan hasn't been in his office all morning."

Too bad because with both Peggy and Carol now missing, Donovan might be the only one left who knew what the heck was going on. "What about Hector? Does he have any idea where Peggy would go and why she'd run?"

"I think it's pretty obvious why she ran," Cooper grumbled. "She's got something to hide." And with another glance at Liam, he believed that *something* was an illegal adoption.

That gave her another jolt of panic and fear.

"I can take Liam upstairs for his nap," her mom offered. Jessa hadn't told her mother about Cooper's suspicions, but she obviously saw the tension between them. Anyone could have, including Liam, and even though her son was young, it wasn't something she wanted him to sense. Especially since he was still recovering from surgery.

Jessa didn't stop her mother from leaving with Liam. She wanted a chance to talk to Cooper alone so she could beg him to, well, she wasn't sure what yet, but she had to do something. It felt as if he was trying to snatch Liam away from her.

"Hector's on the way over here," Cooper added before she could say anything. "He wants to talk to you."

Mercy, that didn't sound good. She prayed he wasn't coming to confess he'd done something illegal to secure Liam's adoption.

"I don't trust Hector," Cooper went on. "So while he's here, I don't want Liam or you alone with him. If he's trying to cover up his part in the adoption, he might consider you both loose ends."

Hearing that spelled out turned her blood to ice, and she forced herself to remember another side of this. "I plan to go through all my recent cases to see if there's someone who could be out for revenge. That might be all this is. Someone who wants to get back at me because I put him or her behind bars."

Cooper nodded, made a sound of mild agreement, but his attention wasn't on her. It was on the two people who came out of the guesthouse about twenty yards away.

Cooper's sister Rayanne and his stepbrother, Seth.

Like the other times Jessa had gotten a glimpse of Seth, he was dressed in a black suit. Very much FBI, and Jessa would have asked for his help if she thought she could trust him.

She couldn't.

Even though Seth and Cooper were at odds, it didn't mean the agent would be willing to help the A.D.A. who had put his adopted mother behind bars.

Rayanne and Seth appeared to be involved in a heavy discussion, but that stopped when they got within earshot of Cooper and her. Cooper's sister threw open the door to the sunroom, stepped in and aimed a glare at Cooper. The glare held when her attention settled on Jessa.

She didn't actually come inside. Rayanne stood in the doorway and ignored the steamy heat that was pouring in around her. "Are you plotting how to keep my mother in jail?" Rayanne snarled.

Jessa wasn't feeling her strongest, but that put some steel in her spine. She nodded. "Because the evidence points to Jewell's guilt."

Rayanne's eyes took on some steel, too, and she got right in Jessa's face. Even though she was Rosalie's twin, there was little resemblance between the two women. Rayanne's eyes were harder, and it didn't help that she looked ready to start a brawl.

One that she could win.

Jessa had heard rumors that Rayanne's boyfriend had dumped her and then been killed. On the very day that she'd learned her mother was about to be arrested for murder. This wasn't exactly a good time in Rayanne's life.

Just like the rest of them.

Cooper stepped between his sister and her. "Jessa's an invited guest in this house," he told Rayanne. "You'll treat her as such."

"Invited," she grumbled. "And I wasn't. If that was meant to insult me, big brother, it won't work." Her index finger landed against Cooper's chest. "I'm staying to make sure you don't team up with your invited houseguest here to put the screws to an innocent woman."

"Rayanne," Seth warned. "Pull your claws back. This is a fight we'll win in court, not here on the ranch. That's the reason I've been telling you to move into the guesthouse, so you won't be under their roof."

Now it was Seth's turn to glare, but his went to Cooper. "Tell me what's going on with the attempt to kidnap the A.D.A.'s son. Is it connected to our mother?"

"Our mother?" Cooper repeated, clearly riled

by that. Maybe because his mother had abandoned him. Maybe because Jewell had adopted Seth.

Maybe both.

There were a lot of reasons for Cooper to be upset, and Jessa could share some of those reasons with him.

"I can't find a connection between this and Jewell," Cooper finally said. "And I don't want you looking for one, either. You'll stay out of my way," he growled.

Seth met him eye to eye. "And you'll stay out of mine."

With that, Seth turned like a sleek jungle cat finished with his prey and walked back toward the guesthouse.

"I know I've already brought this up," Jessa said after Rayanne left, "and you've dismissed it, but what if all of this really is connected to Jewell? Not just the kidnapping attempt but my car accident and Peggy's disappearance."

This time Cooper didn't jump to dismiss it or defend his brothers and father. Nor himself. He just shook his head before his gaze came to hers.

"Someone could be trying to manipulate the investigation. Yeah, I've considered it," he added when she blinked. "Someone could be trying to use Liam to get one of us to tamper with evidence."

And that in turn led back to his mother.

Or maybe to someone who wanted the case against her dropped.

There weren't many people in that camp—Rayanne, Rosalie, Seth and Jewell herself. The only one she could rule out was Rosalie. Yes, it was clear she loved her mother as much as Cooper hated the woman, but Rosalie didn't seem like the sort to cut legal corners, especially when she had her own battle going on—the search for her missing baby.

But maybe someone else had a hand in this.

It wasn't much of a stretch for her to believe someone was trying to tamper with the murder charges against Jewell. After all, someone had stolen or misplaced evidence. Until now, Jessa had figured Cooper or his brothers might have done that, but she had a better understanding of the family dynamics now. The rumors of the rift between mother and sons weren't just rumors. She doubted any of the McKinnon men would lift a finger to help Jewell.

"It's almost as if we're on the same side when it comes to Jewell," she mumbled.

That sent a shot of fire through his eyes. "We might be if you'd quit accusing me of obstruction of justice. I don't care what happens to her. I only care how it affects my father and brothers.

But I wouldn't destroy evidence to keep the mud off us from Jewell's arrest."

No. He wouldn't. She knew that *now*. But knowing it and knowing Cooper better didn't make her situation easier.

"I'm scared," she admitted. And Jessa could tell from the look he gave her that he knew she wasn't just talking about the kidnapping attempt.

Cooper nodded, mumbled some of that profanity he'd held back earlier and reached out. Took her by the arm. And pulled her to him.

Almost immediately she felt him stiffen, and he no doubt would have snapped away from her if Jessa hadn't caught him. Why, she didn't know.

Okay, she did.

It was because that brief moment in his arms had felt darn good. Reassuring. And safe. She hadn't felt safe in days, but it was a mistake to look for that safety in Cooper's arms. And the sound that rumbled in his throat let her know that he agreed.

But he didn't move.

Neither did she.

Jessa just stood there with one of his arms hooked around her. Their gazes met. Held. And she felt that tug again. The one deep in her belly that she didn't want to feel.

"This is *not* going to happen between us," she reminded him, and herself.

The corner of his mouth hitched, and he pulled her even closer to him. Against him. And kissed the top of her head. It was chaste and comforting. Or at least that was what he'd likely intended it to be. But the fire she felt was anything but comforting.

What the heck was wrong with her?

Jessa stepped back. "I have a bad history with men," she said. Then she frowned when Cooper didn't even react to that. It was because he knew about her history, especially the parts she had wanted to keep shut away.

Knew about the nightmare of a relationship that had put her in the emergency room four years ago.

He knew that she'd allowed herself to become a punching bag for a man who'd professed to love her and who had once given her the same tug she was feeling now.

Almost.

This tug for Cooper seemed stronger. Different.

That didn't make it right, and it was no doubt just a response to the danger. In fact, that was all it could be. Even if they semiagreed about Jewell, the trial would still cause trouble between his family and her.

No near smile this time. A muscle flickered in his jaw. "I did read what your ex did to you."

No surprise, but it put a lump in her throat, and the memories of the pain and shame flickered through her.

"I'm sorry," Cooper added.

There it was again. The sympathy fueled the tug. Or maybe Cooper alone was doing that. It was a reminder, a bad one, that it'd been way too long since she'd really been kissed. And Cooper certainly looked as if he knew how to do that.

She felt herself leaning closer to him, and it took her a moment to realize that was because Cooper still had hold of her arm, and he was pulling her back toward him. He was mumbling more profanity, too, as if this was the last thing on earth he wanted to do.

And probably was.

Still, that didn't stop him from touching his lips to hers. Just a quick touch. That went through her like an inferno. She actually lost her breath for a moment.

Her mind, too.

Because she didn't put up a fight to stop what couldn't happen between them. In fact, Jessa was reasonably sure she would have returned the kiss. A real one. Long, slow and deep. If Cooper's phone hadn't buzzed.

He shook his head. Cursed again. And yanked the phone from his pocket.

Jessa stepped back. Way back. And this time

she told that tug to take a hike. Kissing Cooper wasn't just stupid. It was dangerous.

"Your adoption attorney's here," Cooper relayed to her once he'd finished the call.

She certainly hadn't forgotten about Hector's visit, but Jessa hadn't quite braced herself for it. Because this conversation could be dangerous, too, if he ended up admitting that the adoption was illegal.

That gave her the attitude adjustment she needed.

Jessa followed Cooper through the kitchen and to the living room at the front of the house. Hector was standing in the center of the room, and she only needed a glimpse to see the nerves. His tie was askew. Suit coat, too. There were dark circles under his eyes, and his five o'clock shadow was well past the fashionable stage.

"I don't know what you've started," Hector said, his narrowed eyes pinned to her, "but I want it to stop now."

Jessa shook her head. "What are you talking about?"

Hector used the back of his hand to wipe some sweat from his forehead. "Someone broke into my office. They stole my computer and ransacked my files."

Her heart slammed against her chest. "Please tell me you have security cameras."

"No," he mumbled and dropped down onto the sofa. "And no one saw them coming or going. They took your file."

That didn't help her already unsteady breath.

"Anyone else's?" Cooper quickly asked.

"Not that I can tell. Just Jessa's."

Oh, mercy. And that led them right back to an illegal adoption. Or maybe someone who wanted to make it look that way. But Jessa couldn't think of any reason someone would want to do that.

Jessa walked closer, stared down at the man she'd once praised for locating a precious baby for her to adopt. No praise now. She just needed answers. "Do you have any idea where Peggy is?"

"No." Another quick answer. "But she's probably facing the same kind of harassment I am. Now I have an FBI agent calling and demanding to see me."

Cooper and she exchanged glances, but judging from the way Cooper's forehead bunched up, this was the first he was hearing about it, too.

"The agent called a few hours ago, insisted on seeing me and made an appointment for three o'clock. He didn't come out and say it, but it sounds as if I'm under some kind of investigation." His gaze snapped to Cooper now. "What the hell did you say or do to get me into this mess?"

"I didn't say or do anything. I want the name of the agent," Cooper insisted without pausing.

"Gordon Riker. Why? You don't trust him?"

"No, I don't. Don't trust you, either. But in the case of the agent, he could be a fake. If you're not the one trying to cover up an illegal adoption, then maybe this person is."

That brought Hector to his feet. "I'm not covering up anything, and I won't have my livelihood destroyed with questions and accusations from the two of you."

"I'll ask all the questions I want to get to the truth." Cooper went to Jessa's side, and the look he shot Hector was a lot more intimidating than one she could have managed. Added to the fact that Cooper towered over Hector.

"Was anything about this adoption illegal?" Cooper demanded.

"No." Hector made another swipe at the beads of sweat popping out all over his face. "And from now on, you'll communicate with me only through my attorney." He extracted a card from his pocket and dropped it on the coffee table.

Hector started to leave but then stopped and looked at Jessa. "I don't deserve this."

"Neither does Liam." Her voice cracked, and Jessa hoped she didn't lose it before she could get her point across. "My baby's in danger, and I need to find out why."

Even if it would crush her heart, she had to know. She couldn't go on like this, with a threat hanging over his head.

Hector closed his eyes a moment. "I don't know why, but I swear to you, it had nothing to do with me."

Now he walked out, and while his parting line had sounded reassuring, it wasn't. Hector had earned plenty of money from Liam's adoption, and he'd handled several others that same month. The cash alone was motive enough to cut corners.

"Have you asked for a check of Hector's financial records?" Jessa asked.

"Yeah." Cooper went to the front window and watched Hector get back in his sleek silver sports car. "Not just him, either. I've asked for checks on everyone involved in this."

"Including me?" Jessa mumbled.

He glanced back at her. "You, too. I would apologize, but you'd do the same in my position."

Jessa couldn't deny that. She would. But considering that almost kiss they'd just shared, it seemed uncomfortable. Like sleeping with the enemy. Too bad she was deeply attracted to this enemy. Also too bad that this particular enemy could end up crushing her heart worse than it'd ever been crushed.

His phone buzzed, and while Cooper continued to watch Hector drive away, he answered it without glancing at the screen. However, he quickly did a double take.

"Donovan?" Cooper spat out like profanity. "I've been looking… What?"

That got her moving closer to Cooper so she could hear what had put that stunned look on his face. "Let me talk to her," Cooper said a moment later.

Her?

Jessa moved even closer, but she only caught a word here and there. It wasn't a woman's voice she heard but rather a man's. A scared one, from the sound of it. The moments crawled by, and the man continued to chatter.

"Too risky," Cooper finally said.

She missed the man's answer, but whatever it was, it turned every muscle in Cooper's body to iron. Then he cursed. "I'll be there in thirty minutes. Don't make me regret this, or you're a dead man."

"What's wrong?" Jessa asked the moment he put his phone away.

"Donovan said Peggy's at his ranch, and she's holding him at gunpoint. And if we don't go out there now, Peggy says she'll kill him."

Chapter Eight

Cooper stopped at the foot of the circular driveway that led to Donovan's house. The place sprawled across the top of a hill, and even though he'd never been inside it, he figured there were at least thirty rooms. Too many places for Peggy to be holding Donovan at gunpoint.

If that was really what was going on.

As far as Cooper was concerned, both Donovan and Peggy were suspects in this mess of an investigation, and he couldn't rule out that they had partnered up to lure Jessa and him to Donovan's ranch.

Or maybe this was a ploy to separate him from Liam and Jessa.

No matter which way he went, it could be a huge risk, but since he was the sheriff and a man in need of answers, it was a risk he had to take. Still, he'd taken precautions and left Tucker and a dozen armed ranch hands to guard Liam.

Jessa was a different story.

She'd refused to stay, insisting that she come with him as Peggy had demanded. Jessa had even played her A.D.A. card and claimed she needed to question both Donovan and Peggy. Since their argument had eaten up precious time, Cooper had decided to take the most hardheaded woman in the state with him. That didn't mean he had any intention of letting her get close to what could turn out to be a hostage situation.

"Wait here," Cooper growled.

"I could maybe help," Jessa argued.

"Yeah, by doing as I say and staying put." Cooper looked at his deputy Reed, who'd just pulled up behind them and gotten out of his vehicle. "And you stay with her. If she tries to come in before I give the all clear, arrest her."

Oh, she didn't like that. Jessa hurled little eyeball daggers at him, but Cooper just hurled them right back. Jessa had taken enough chances just by coming here.

He waited until Colt had parked his truck, and the two started for the house. Not a direct route where they'd be in the line of fire. Cooper used some hedges for cover. However, he and Colt had only made it a few steps when his phone buzzed again. Donovan's name was on the screen, but it was Peggy's voice he heard when he answered and put the call on speaker.

"Bring Jessa Wells in with you," Peggy demanded. "I want you both to hear the truth from this lying—"

"Jessa's staying put," Cooper interrupted. "Once you've surrendered your gun and I'm sure it's safe, I'll let her in."

"Stop arguing with this nutcase!" Donovan yelled. "Get in here and do your job."

Cooper's jaw clenched. "My job doesn't mean putting a civilian in danger. Jessa stays put. Now, where are you two?"

"The foyer," Peggy answered. "The door's unlocked. And don't try anything stupid because I'm watching you on a security camera."

So that was how she'd known that Jessa wasn't making her way to the house. It also meant that ducking behind the hedges wouldn't do any good. Of course, if Peggy wanted him dead, she would have already fired.

Cooper looked up the steps to the porch, where there was a trio of front doors with panels of beveled glass. The light caught the bevels just right, making it hard for him to see more than shadows on the other side. He didn't know which one was Peggy.

"Where's the staff? Is anyone hurt?" Cooper asked.

"No one's hurt." Peggy again. "Not yet, anyway. I searched the place, and I only found two maids. I made them get on the floor. If their boss moves, I start shooting."

Hell. So not just one hostage, but three.

"She had me call my ranch hands," Donovan volunteered. "She had me give the same warning to them as she did to the maids. Personally, I'm hoping one of them or you will put a bullet in her."

Cooper heard a sound. A hoarse sob, and it took him a second to realize it was Peggy crying. "You have to believe me. I didn't steal any babies."

"I'm listening." Cooper forced his voice to stay calm.

Hard to do though with the whirlwind of emotions whipping through him. Because this showdown could lead to info about Liam. It could also get him shot. Jessa, too. And that was why he had to defuse things before they got any worse.

"Peggy, if you'll put down your gun and come outside, I'll listen to everything you want to tell me," Cooper assured her.

"What she wants to tell you is a pack of lies!" Donovan shouted. "I didn't steal a kid." Cooper didn't think it was his imagination that the man sounded a lot more riled than afraid.

"Like I said, I'll listen to her," Cooper went on. "And if she convinces me that you've done something wrong, then I'll arrest you."

"I'll kill you before I let you arrest me," Donovan fired back.

Cooper huffed. That was their old rivalry rearing its ugly head, and he didn't have time for it now. If Donovan needed arresting, it *would* happen.

"Peggy, put down your gun and release your hostage," Cooper repeated. "If you're as innocent as you say, then you'll have a chance to prove it. And I'll help you."

Silence. For a long time. "Give your phone to Jessa," Peggy finally said. "I need to tell her something."

Cooper looked back at Jessa, who was already hurrying closer. Reed managed to get a hand on her shoulder, but that didn't stop her from shouting out to Peggy.

"I'm here," Jessa assured her. "And I'm listening."

Peggy made another of those hoarse sobs. "I have files that'll prove where I got the babies. I brought them with me."

"And I'll read them," Jessa promised, walking even closer to the phone. "Just please put down your gun so that no one gets hurt."

More silence, but Cooper hoped Peggy was at least considering surrendering. The woman didn't say a word, but several moments later, the front door eased open.

Cooper took aim in case Peggy came out shooting, but it wasn't Peggy. With his hands raised in the air, Donovan stepped out onto the porch. He looked pretty darn calm and collected for a hostage. There wasn't a strand of his dark blond hair out of place. Ditto for his expensive-looking dark blue business suit. But there was one thing off.

His hands were tied.

"The dingbat still has a gun trained on me, and she's accusing Carol and me of being involved with illegal adoptions," Donovan said though clenched teeth. His steely gaze met Cooper's, and the man had the gall to smirk. "A good sheriff could have prevented this," he added.

"Living a clean life could have prevented it, too. Or maybe just a good security system."

"She came in with the trash." Donovan's smirk softened a bit, replaced by a scowl aimed back in Peggy's direction. "I had the gate open so the trashmen could come in, and she drove in right behind their truck. I didn't see her until it was too late."

Clearly, Donovan wasn't pleased about Peggy getting the drop on him, but he was aiming just as much displeasure at Cooper.

"Peggy?" Cooper called out. "Your turn now. Come to the door so I can see you."

Cooper held his breath and hoped like the devil

that the woman would cooperate. Then he could question both Donovan and her and get a look at the files that she said she had.

But she didn't answer. She certainly didn't do anything to surrender her gun.

"Peggy?" Cooper called out again.

And her name had hardly left his mouth when he heard a sound he didn't want to hear.

A shot blasted through the air.

JESSA'S STOMACH WENT to her knees.

She didn't have time to react to the shot before Cooper came running toward her, yelling for her to get down.

Everything seemed to happen at once. Peggy gave a bloodcurdling scream. Cooper dragged Jessa to the ground behind some massive landscape boulders. Donovan jumped off the side of the porch and into some shrubs. And Cooper and his deputies all took aim at the house.

God, why had Peggy fired the shot?

The woman had already gotten everyone's attention by taking Donovan hostage. She hadn't needed to do anything else so drastic.

"Peggy!" Cooper shouted. "Put down your gun and come out with your hands up."

She didn't answer, but Donovan did. The man started cursing, calling Peggy all kinds of names. Jessa couldn't blame him. Peggy had broken into his home and held him at gunpoint, but then maybe she'd done that because Donovan deserved having a gun pointed at him. Still, Jessa kept going back to the same question: How would Donovan have gotten Liam in the first place?

He ran a very successful cattle-broker business and was filthy rich. There was no need for him to get involved with adoptions.

Unless Liam's adoption was somehow personal for him.

Considering his history with Cooper, it could very well be that, but it still didn't make sense.

Another shot rang out; this time the bullet struck the cement just yards from them. Cooper moved her, pushing her behind the truck, and looked around. Not at the front of the house.

But at the roof.

"The shot came from up there," Cooper mumbled.

Because her heartbeat was crashing in her ears, it took Jessa a moment to realize something wasn't right about that, either. How could Peggy have made it from the foyer to the roof so quickly?

And then she got her answer when she caught a glimpse of the man dressed in black. He was armed with a rifle, and he leaned out of one of the dormer windows.

Definitely not Peggy.

That meant she'd brought along some help.

But then, why had she screamed?

Another shot came at them. Then another. The deputies scrambled behind Colt's truck, using it for cover. Cooper pushed Jessa even lower to the ground, but he didn't follow suit. He levered himself up and fired.

The shot was deafening, and the tinny echoes clanged in Jessa's head. Still, it was worth it if Cooper stopped this monster.

But he didn't.

The shooter fired several more shots, each of them ricocheting off Cooper's truck and nearby boulders. She prayed none of the shots hit anyone.

After what seemed an eternity, the shots stopped. Jessa sucked in her breath, waited. Prayed some more, too. But the shooter didn't pull the trigger again.

"Stay put," Cooper warned her, and he motioned for Reed to move behind the truck with her.

The moment his deputy was in place, Cooper and Colt began to inch their way to the house. They kept cover behind the shrubs, but Jessa knew that wouldn't give them much protection from bullets.

"You stay down, too," Cooper said, and she figured he was talking to Donovan.

The man obviously didn't listen.

"I know you're not deaf," Cooper growled, "so that makes you stupid. Stay down!"

"It's my house," Donovan argued. "Besides, I want to get my hands around that witch's neck."

Jessa heard a thudding sound, and she peered around Reed's shoulder to see Donovan tumbling onto the porch. Judging from Cooper's body language, he'd been the one to put him there. He turned his gun on Donovan when the man started to get up.

Donovan stayed put.

But he gave Cooper a glare that would make Hades freeze over.

There were stone inserts between the glass doors, and Cooper used one of them for cover. "Peggy?" he tried again.

Still no answer.

He said something to Colt that she didn't catch, and a split second later, the two pivoted into the partially open doorway. They looked inside.

And both cursed.

"She's gone," Cooper relayed to Reed.

That brought Donovan to his feet. He'd managed to get his hands untied, and he flung the rope aside and barreled into the foyer. Cooper stopped him from going any farther.

"Get Jessa inside," Cooper told Reed. "In case the shooter is headed your way."

That put her heart right back in her throat, and both Colt and Cooper became backup for Reed as he hurried her inside. Cooper immediately positioned her so that her back was to the wall and he was in front of her. Protecting her again.

Jessa looked around the massive foyer and the equally massive rooms that flanked it.

No sign of Peggy.

Just two terrified-looking women in maids' uniforms. They were on the white-carpeted floor in the living room.

"She ran toward the back," one of them said.

Cooper tipped his head for Colt and Reed to go in that direction. "Find her. The shooter, too. They're probably escaping together."

"She's not going anywhere," Donovan snapped, and he would have followed Reed and Colt if Cooper hadn't grabbed a handful of Donovan's jacket.

"Start talking," Cooper ordered.

Donovan threw off his grip and looked on the verge of throwing a punch. His nostrils flared. Eyes narrowed. But then he stepped back and shot Cooper another of those smirks that made Jessa want to slug him. That was no doubt the reason he'd used it—because she could tell it infuriated Cooper, too.

"Start talking?" Donovan coolly repeated. He

adjusted his jacket and brushed off some bits of the shrubs as if he had all the time in the world. "Why should I respond to that woman's lies? Peggy's clearly mentally unbalanced. You sure she's not a relative of yours?" he asked, looking at Cooper. "Insanity seems to run in your family. Killers, too."

If Cooper had any reaction to that, he didn't show it. "Why would Peggy say you were the one who gave her the baby that Jessa adopted?"

Donovan lifted his shoulder. "Mentally unbalanced people say a lot of things that aren't true. I can't believe you'd listen to a word she said."

"She said she had proof," Cooper reminded him.

"Where?" He lifted his hands, palms up. Then he leaned in. "You shouldn't believe everything crazy people say."

"I didn't say I believed her. I just want a straight answer. Did you give Peggy a baby that was meant to be adopted?"

They got into a staring contest that crawled on and on. Donovan was the first to break eye contact, and he laughed. "Me with a baby? Really? Do I look like the baby-handling type? I'm not, and if Molly were alive, she'd vouch for me on that."

Because Jessa had her hand on Cooper's back,

she felt his muscles go stiff. "What the hell does that mean?" Cooper snapped.

"You want me to spell it out? Well, here it is. Molly and I were lovers—"

"And she broke off things with you and eventually married me," Cooper interrupted. "Old water, old bridge. Why bring her up now?"

"Simple. I was just making a reference. Molly knew I wasn't the daddy type, and that's why she eventually left me and went to you. Because she knew you'd give her a kid."

Cooper gave him a flat look. "I think you glossed over a few things, like Molly realizing you're a jerk and ending a toxic relationship."

Donovan lifted his shoulder, adjusted his suit again. "Obviously, she told you a different version of the truth. If I gave up Molly over my no-kid rule, then why the heck would I want to get into the baby business?"

"I don't know," Cooper fired back. "Why don't you tell me?"

"There's nothing to tell. Even if I'd wanted to be part of the *wonderful world* of adoption, why would I go looking for some kid to give to a whack job like Peggy? If I wanted to make money selling black-market babies, I sure as hell wouldn't use her for a middleman."

He sounded convincing, but Jessa didn't trust

him. She certainly hadn't liked the way he'd thrown his relationship with Molly in Cooper's face.

"You need to come with me to the sheriff's office," Cooper said, sounding all business now. But Jessa could still feel his knotted muscles.

"I don't have time to play cop with you." Donovan smirked again.

Cooper didn't back down. "You'll make time. Several felonies were committed here, and that means paperwork."

Donovan stared at him, again looking as if he might challenge Cooper's authority. And he might have done just that. If they hadn't heard the footsteps.

Colt and Reed hurried back in, both shaking their heads. "No sign of Peggy or the shooter," Colt relayed.

"Great, just great," Donovan snarled. "You let them get away."

Cooper didn't even spare him a glance. He kept his attention on his brother. "What is that?"

Jessa had to go on her tiptoes to see over his shoulder, and she spotted what appeared to be a piece of paper in Colt's left hand.

Colt unfolded it and held up a flash drive. "I found it in the kitchen on the counter by the back door. Peggy left it." He looked down at the writing on the paper, then shook his head. "The note's addressed to you, Jessa."

Cooper reached out and took the note from his brother. Jessa quickly moved to his side so she could see what was written there.

Ms. Wells, the answers about the adoption are somewhere in these files. Read them and you'll learn the truth about your son.

Chapter Nine

Cooper's eyes were burning, but he forced himself to keep reading the computer files that Peggy had left on the flash drive. Jessa was doing the same on another laptop that she'd positioned on the other side of his desk in his home office.

"Anything?" he asked when she made a soft sound. But he quickly realized it was a sound of frustration.

"Nothing." She checked the time, glanced at the baby monitor that she'd brought downstairs and mumbled something about Liam waking up from his nap soon. Jessa would want to check on him. Cooper would, too.

"Did you find anything?" she asked.

He had to shake his head. Nothing in the thirtysomething files he'd already gone through, but they had twice that to go. It wasn't as straightforward as Cooper had thought it would be, because Peggy's adoption notes read more like a disorganized personal diary of her feelings over the placements that she'd helped arrange.

But she hadn't used names.

And sometimes she'd handled several adoptions at the same time and had merged those notes with ramblings of why she preferred one set of prospective parents over another.

That meant wading through page after page and trying to figure out which of the babies was Liam.

Read them and you'll learn the truth about your son, Peggy had said in her note. Cooper only hoped she was telling the truth about that.

His phone buzzed, and Cooper answered it right away when he saw Colt's name on the screen. He also put it on speaker because Jessa looked as ready for news, any news, as he was.

"Please tell me you found Peggy." Part of him wanted to be out looking for her himself, but that wouldn't be wise, since it would leave Jessa and Liam without protection. Besides, someone had to go through Peggy's files, and the people with the highest stakes in that potential info were Jessa and him.

"No sign of her, but I followed some footprints I found at the back of Donovan's house, and they led to a heavily treed area. I'm pretty sure the footprints were hers and that's where she'd left a vehicle, because there were tire tracks."

Yeah. And it was reminder for Cooper that he'd screwed this up big time. He should have moved one of his deputies to the rear of the house to prevent Peggy and the gunman from escaping. But he truly hadn't believed it was an actual hostage situation. In fact, he'd thought Donovon and Peggy might have been in on this ruse together.

"There's more," Colt said. "I found a second set of footprints and tire tracks on the east side of the property. Judging from the size of the footprints, they probably belong to the shooter."

Jessa's gaze met his, and he saw the question there in her eyes. Why hadn't Peggy and her hired gun driven to Donovan's together?

And that brought him back to the first shot that'd been fired.

"Peggy had screamed," Cooper said, thinking aloud. "And it didn't sound fake, either. It sounded like the reaction of a woman who'd been surprised. Terrified, even. So why would she have reacted like that if she'd known all along what was going to happen?"

"Maybe her hired goon jumped the gun and wasn't supposed to shoot?" Jessa suggested.

It was a good theory, but Cooper had another possibility that only created more questions than answers. "Or maybe the hired gun wasn't working for her. Maybe he was working for Donovan."

"Or he could have been working with our hospitalized gunman, Vernon Graham," Jessa added. "Think about it—Graham is the one who implicated Peggy, and she in turn said Donovan was guilty. All this finger-pointing muddies the waters and might be leading us in the wrong direction."

"The direction of illegal adoptions," Cooper finished for her. "But if it's not about the adoptions, then it takes us back to Jewell or some other case that could cause someone to go off the deep end like this."

Colt made a sound of agreement. "I found something else at the second scene," Colt went on. "A scuff mark on one of the trees near the tracks. Looks like the vehicle ran into it while the driver was making an escape. I got some black paint chips. Already sent those to the lab. We might get lucky identifying the type of vehicle."

Yes, and maybe that would in turn lead them to the driver.

"Tucker's putting out feelers in case the driver brings the vehicle in for repairs," Colt added. "I'll go back to the hospital and have another chat with Graham. When I'm finished with him, I'll see how Reed is faring with Donovan."

Cooper doubted Donovan would say anything of importance, and the man darn sure wouldn't incriminate himself. In fact, Cooper knew from Reed's earlier call that Donovan had lawyered up before he'd even stepped foot in the sheriff's office.

"When you talk to Donovan, ask him how a gunman could have gotten on his roof without him knowing about it," Cooper said. "His place has to have state-of-the-art security, and I find it hard to believe that Donovan or his staff didn't hear or see anyone suspicious."

"Will do," Colt assured him.

"What about the FBI agent that Hector Dixon said had contacted him? Gordon Riker. Any luck talking to him?"

With everything else going on, Jessa had forgotten all about the man. Thankfully, Cooper hadn't.

"He doesn't exist," Colt said. "Well, he doesn't exist by that name, anyway. So either Hector made him up or else someone called him using an alias. Someone who maybe wanted to feel him out and find out how much he knows."

Yes, and maybe silence him if he knew too much. Of course, Hector had likely heard what'd happened with Peggy at Donovan's house, so hopefully the man was being more vigilant. If he was innocent, that was.

"You making any progress with Peggy's files?" Colt asked.

"None," Jessa and he said in unison.

"But I think we should do a deeper background check on Peggy," Jessa continued. Then she paused. "Because I'm not sure we're dealing with someone who's mentally stable."

She looked at Cooper as if he might disagree, but he couldn't. Maybe Peggy just had a bad case of attention deficient when it came to her notes, but she certainly rambled a lot. And so far there was nothing of importance. However, it did make Cooper wonder how Peggy had gotten started in this whole baby-brokering operation. She didn't seem to have a lot of business sense, or any other sense, for that matter.

"I'll ask Tucker to do another background check," Colt said. "Unless you want me to involve the FBI in this."

The image of Seth and his mirrored shades popped into Cooper's head. "No. We'll keep this between us for now."

Cooper ended the call and went back to the notes. But he didn't get far. He heard sounds coming over the baby monitor. Not a cry exactly, but Liam seemed to be fussing. A glance at the screen and Cooper saw the little boy moving around in the crib. It got Jessa to her feet, and with Cooper right behind her, she hurried out of his office.

"Sometimes, when he first wakes up, he picks at the bandage," Jessa said from over her shoulder.

That was a good reason for her to hurry, especially since her mother had told them she'd be in the kitchen with Rosalie and the cook. But Cooper thought Jessa's urgency had just as much to do with this latest attack. She was terrified for Liam's safety.

Jessa practically ran once she reached the top of the stairs, but she stopped in the doorway. That sent a jolt of concern through him, but when Cooper reached the door, Jessa put her index finger to her lip.

"He went back to sleep," she whispered.

She didn't move, and neither did Cooper. They stood there and watched. Well, until Jessa looked up at him. And frowned. Probably because the emotion was written all over his face every time he looked at the little boy. Jessa wasn't the only one who was worried for Liam's safety.

And his future.

"I don't want this," she said, moving from the door. She leaned her back against the wall opposite the guest room where Liam was sleeping.

No need for her to qualify what *this* was. If she had her way, she'd shut Cooper out of Liam's life. Cooper understood that, but he wasn't going anywhere.

"I should leave," she added a moment later. "I

should hire some bodyguards to protect us in a safe, hidden location."

He could see the panic starting to bubble up inside her. Cooper wasn't about to dismiss that, either. But he also couldn't let her do anything stupid.

Cooper took her hand when she reached in her pocket for her phone. "You're both safe here."

She huffed when her gaze dropped to the grip he had on her, and jerked away from him. But she didn't reach for her phone again and she didn't tell him to keep the heck away from her son.

"I just need this to be over," she said, her voice breaking on the last word. "If we knew who was behind the attacks, then we'd know how to stop them."

"Yeah," Cooper settled for saying. And because she looked as if she needed it in the worst way, he hooked his arm around her neck and pulled her into a hug.

Now she resisted. She put her palms on his chest as if to push him away. That didn't happen, either. A small sob sounded in her throat, and she dropped her head to his shoulder.

"It's not right for me to be here like this," Jessa mumbled.

He couldn't argue with that. It wasn't right even if it felt like it was. Because when Cooper caught the jerk responsible for the attacks and put him behind bars, there would still be unsettled issues with Jessa. His mother's murder trial, for one. These ever-growing feelings he had for Liam, for another.

And finally, the attraction between Jessa and him.

He seriously doubted it was just going to vanish when the danger ended. It certainly wasn't going anywhere now.

"Let's just get it over with," he said.

Her gaze snapped to his, and before she could ask if he'd lost his bloomin' mind—which was a strong possibility—Cooper put his mouth on hers. He caught the slight sound of surprise she made. Caught her scent and taste, too. All in all, it was enough to prove he was stupid to play with this kind of fire.

Did that stop him?

Nope.

He just kept on kissing her. Kept on reining her in, closer and closer, until Jessa was plastered against him.

Cooper deepened the kiss. Waited for her to stop him. And waited some more. During that wait, he didn't let up, and when he had Jessa gasping for air, he dropped some kisses on her neck.

And got a darn good response.

Well, it was a good one if his intentions were for this to continue. She made a sound. A silky little hitch in her voice that came from deep within her throat. But that wasn't all. She slid her arms around his neck and pulled him down so she could do some kiss deepening of her own.

Oh, man. They'd both lost it.

Not good. Cooper had figured the attraction would get the best of them, but he'd hoped that the craziness would be limited to one at a time. So the other could do something to stop it.

Neither of them was stopping anything.

Somewhere way in the back of his mind, Cooper reminded himself that they were in the hall. Where they could easily be seen. He wanted to keep kissing Jessa. Hell, he wanted to haul her off to bed. Not only was that a really bad idea, but the timing also sucked.

Obviously coming to her senses, too, she stopped kissing him at the same time he stopped kissing her and they backed away from each other.

She opened her mouth. Closed it. Opened it again and then shook her head. "Why?"

Since that could encompass a lot of different areas, Cooper just shrugged. And waited. Jessa would no doubt lecture him on why kissing was totally inappropriate and a judicial conflict of interest.

But she didn't.

She swallowed hard. "You read what happened in my last relationship, and you know I'm not ready for this."

He nodded and rubbed his thumb over the back of his left ring finger, where he used to wear his wedding band. It wasn't there now. Not physically. It was in the nightstand drawer next to his bed. But there were times when he still felt plenty married.

Not now, of course.

But other times.

Funny though—those times seemed farther and farther apart since Jessa had stormed into his life.

"We should make a pact or something," she said. "To make sure this doesn't happen again."

Cooper lifted his eyebrow. He was about to remind her that no pact would have prevented what just happened when his phone buzzed. Maybe this time it'd be Colt with news that they'd found Peggy or that Donovan had confessed to a felony or two.

But it wasn't Colt.

It was Dr. Howland.

"Cooper," the doc said the moment Cooper answered. But then he paused. "There was a break-in at the lab where I sent Liam's and your DNA.

There's security footage, so you might be able to find out who did it, but the bottom line is the samples were destroyed. Someone set fire to them."

Hell. He didn't want to go through asking Jessa for another sample, but that was minor compared to the big picture. The person who'd destroyed the samples had likely done so in order to cover something up. And that brought Cooper right back to Peggy, Hector and Donovan.

Jessa, too.

She probably hadn't heard exactly what Dr. Howland had just said, but she could no doubt see the change in Cooper's body language. She knew something was wrong.

"We'll need to repeat the DNA test," Cooper said to the doc.

Jessa made a soft, helpless sound and touched her fingers to her suddenly quivering lips.

"No need to repeat it," Dr. Howland insisted. "I sent out two sets of samples. The first was the one that was destroyed. I used fake names on the second set and sent them to a different lab. Considering everything that was going on with Jessa and that car accident, I thought it was for the best."

Everything inside Cooper went still.

"And?" Cooper asked the doctor, though he

wasn't sure how he was able to speak now that his throat had clamped shut.

Dr. Howland cleared his throat. "I just got back the DNA results...."

Chapter Ten

Jessa watched as Cooper staggered back a step. His breath was gusting now, and he squeezed his eyes shut.

"You're positive?" Cooper asked the caller, his voice hoarse and raw.

She'd seen Dr. Howland's name on the phone screen and had thought he was calling to check on Liam. No such luck. There was only one thing that could have caused Cooper to react like that.

The DNA test was back.

Jessa waited, her own breath racing. Cooper finally hit the end-call button, but it took a moment for his gaze to come to hers.

And she knew in her heart what the doctor had just told him.

That Liam's DNA was a match to his.

"No!" Jessa frantically shook her head and kept repeating it because she didn't know what else to say.

She turned to bolt away from him so she could

take Liam…and do what, exactly, she wasn't sure. However, everything inside her was screaming for her to run, and that was exactly what she would have done if Cooper hadn't caught her arm.

"You can't go," Cooper insisted.

The emotions slammed into her all at once. The fear. Denial. The sickening dread. "You're lying. The doctor's lying. Liam can't be yours. Because he's mine!"

She tried to bolt again, and this time Cooper took her by the shoulders and put her against the wall. He got right in her face.

"Think this through," he said, not easily. Like hers, his words sounded strangled. "Doc Howland did the test, not me, and he has no motive for lying about the results."

"He's your friend!"

"And he's honest. He wouldn't even do the test without a court order."

That tore at her heart like jabs from a razor-sharp knife. Jessa didn't want logic. She wanted the results to prove that Cooper's suspicions had been wrong. Because if they were right… oh, God.

Then he would have a claim to Liam.

The sob made its way up her throat, and Jessa batted away Cooper's hands when he tried to hold her in place.

"Just stop a minute," Cooper said.

Her gaze snapped to his, and that was when Jessa saw something that she didn't want to see. The emotions rifling through him, too. His were a different kind, though. While he was coming to terms with learning his son was alive, she was faced with the nightmare of losing Liam.

"You can't take him from me," she argued. But she was arguing with herself.

Cooper's grip melted off her, and, forcing out several deep breaths, he leaned against the wall. Probably because his legs looked ready to buckle. He had his attention fastened to Liam, who was thankfully still asleep.

He shook his head. "I'd given up. But I shouldn't have. I kept feeling something." He rapped his fist against his heart. "Something kept telling me he was alive. I couldn't allow myself to believe it."

Each word crushed her. "I've been his mother since he was three months old," she said in a whisper.

"I know." He drew in a long breath and walked to the doorway, no doubt so he could get a better look at Liam.

Sweet heaven.

Cooper no doubt saw himself in Liam's face.

Jessa didn't want to see it. Just as she hadn't

wanted to question why Liam had Cooper's rare blood type. She hadn't wanted to question anything.

She'd only wanted her son.

"He's awake," Cooper said a split second before she heard Liam stirring in the crib.

Both Cooper and she moved toward him, but Jessa made it to him first and scooped him up in her arms. She held him to her as if her life depended on it. Because that was exactly how she felt.

"How could this have happened?" Cooper mumbled.

Jessa had to shake her head again. "I got references for the adoption attorney. I followed the rules. I didn't do anything wrong."

"I didn't do anything wrong, either." Cooper reached out, skimmed his finger down Liam's cheek. Liam smiled, breaking her heart even more. "But someone did."

"Maybe not." Her heart was pounding, and she was still breathing too fast. So fast she might hyperventilate. Jessa tried to tamp down her emotions so she could think of a way out of this.

She couldn't lose Liam. That wasn't an option.

But the tears and the doubts came, anyway. And she cursed them. Silently cursed, too, the footsteps she heard in the hall. She didn't want to see anyone right now, including Cooper, though she figured he wasn't going away.

Tucker stepped into the doorway, his attention going straight to his brother. "You okay?" His gaze swept from Cooper to Liam to her.

"I had a DNA test run on Liam," Cooper said. "It's a match to mine."

She had no idea how much he'd told his brother, but apparently not much, since Tucker seemed genuinely surprised. He gasped and caught the doorjamb. "But how? Molly and Cameron washed away in the flood."

"Only Molly." A moment later, Cooper repeated it.

"Well, that explains the phone call I just got from Colt," Tucker went on. "He said he's reviewing some security feed for a break-in at Merritt Labs. He's already got the footage, thanks to Doc Howland."

Cooper nodded. "Someone destroyed the samples of Liam's and my DNA at that particular lab." He paused. Touched Liam's cheek again. "Whoever destroyed those samples is no doubt trying to cover up their part in the illegal adoption."

Oh, God. And it was maybe the reason the kidnappers had tried to take Liam from the hospital.

"Help Colt go through the footage," Cooper told his brother. "Find out who did this." He turned his head, his eyes meeting Tucker's. "We might be looking for a killer."

Tucker nodded as if he'd already figured that out, but Jessa had to shake her head. "You think this person murdered Molly?"

"He or she got their hands on Liam somehow." Cooper's jaw tightened. "No way would Molly have just let someone take him from her."

He hadn't said that easily, and despite the emotional pain crushing her chest, Jessa could practically feel Cooper's pain, too.

"The autopsy proved that drowning was the cause of her death," Tucker reminded him. He came closer and put his hand on his brother's arm. "And there were no signs of foul play."

"Maybe because the foul play was the drowning itself. Someone could have kidnapped Liam...Cameron," Cooper corrected, "and then restrained Molly somehow and moved the car to the bridge so it'd be swept away with her inside."

Jessa couldn't argue with that. Though she wanted to. She wanted to dismiss all of this, but she couldn't.

She looked at her son. Really looked at him. At his eyes. His hair. The shape of his face. Liam seemed puzzled by the intense scrutiny he was getting from all three of them. Well, for a few moments, anyway.

"Horsey," Liam said, and he motioned toward

the plastic horse in the toy box. The last thing Jessa wanted to do was let go of him, but when Liam continued to twist and squirm, she set him on the floor and he made a beeline for the toy chest.

It hit her then. The toys and the crib had almost certainly belonged to Cameron. When she'd first arrived at the ranch, she hadn't even questioned why these things would be there.

"I can't stay here," Jessa blurted out.

The brothers exchanged a quick glance, and Tucker headed for the door. "I'll see if Colt's making progress with the security footage from the lab."

Cooper didn't say a word to her until Tucker had left. "We need a truce. Right now our focus has to be keeping Liam safe, agreed?"

Jessa didn't have to think about that. She nodded. "But you can't take him from me," she repeated, positioning herself between Liam and him.

It didn't work. Cooper just moved around her and sat on the floor next to Liam. Her son obviously enjoyed having a new playmate, because he smiled and handed Cooper a toy from the box.

"A truce," Cooper repeated. "You won't try to take him from this house, and I won't do anything to take him from you."

Not now, anyway.

Cooper hadn't actually said those words, but she could hear them in his voice.

"Say that you'll agree to a truce," Cooper added. Even though it was an order—she had no doubts about that—he smiled back at Liam.

It was the last thing she wanted to say, but the only thing she could do. If she tried to leave with Liam, Cooper would stop her. Legally, Liam was still hers, but Cooper could change that by filing a motion for custody.

Which he would no doubt do once Liam was safe.

"Truce," Jessa finally managed to say, just as Cooper's phone rang.

Cooper continued to play with Liam while he took out his phone. Jessa saw Colt's name on the screen, and even though Cooper took the call on speaker, she sank down next to him so she could hear better. And so she could better monitor this playing session. Yes, she was being petty again, but it was the only control she had over this nightmare of a situation.

"I've got good news and bad," Colt started. "The bad is that whoever broke into Merritt Lab also disabled the camera. Not sure how, but it looks like some kind of electromagnetic device."

Cooper looked ready to curse. He didn't. Probably because of Liam. "You said there's good news?"

"Yeah. There's no footage of the person in the lab, but I got a picture of him or her stepping from the vehicle. It's just the one shot because the camera was disabled immediately afterward."

"Please tell me you got the license plate numbers," Cooper said.

"No, it was obscured with something, but I have a good description of the vehicle. A late-model black Jeep Cherokee with some damage to the front right fender. That's a match to the paint chips that I found near Donovan's place."

So the person who fired those shots had likely broken into the lab.

"We're running the names of all owners of that particular vehicle model," Colt went on. "We might get lucky."

"What about the interview with Donovan?" Cooper asked. "You get anything?"

"Nothing. His lawyer advised him to stay quiet, and that's what he's done. I'm about to cut him loose."

"Not yet," Cooper argued. "I'll come in and talk to him."

Colt hesitated. "You're sure? Because it seems to me you got other things on your mind right now."

"I need to help. I need to end this so that Liam's no longer in danger."

Jessa wanted that, too. Desperately wanted it.

But with the kidnapper caught and behind bars, it would leave Cooper free to pursue custody of Liam.

"All right," Colt finally said. "I'll email you all the updates and files so you can read them before you come in."

Cooper thanked him, ended the call and went back to playing with Liam. When Liam made a neighing sound with the toy horse, Cooper mimicked it, causing Liam to laugh.

"He's always been fascinated by horses," Jessa mumbled.

"Once he's all healed, we'll have to get him out to the pasture to see some real ones." Cooper looked up at her, maybe waiting for her to say that wouldn't happen, that she would be long gone by then.

"Remember that truce," she mumbled.

"I am. I'm remembering that kiss, too."

Jessa flinched. "What does that have to do with anything?"

Cooper gave her a flat look. "Everything, and you know it. If it weren't for this attraction between us, I would have already made a call to start custody proceedings."

Yes, she did know that. And it terrified her even more. Because what would happen when this attraction ended? She wasn't sure what troubled her most—that it would end...

Or that it wouldn't.

Jessa had no idea what she would do then—feeling this heat with the man who could destroy her.

Cooper's phone buzzed again, but this time she didn't recognize the name she saw on the screen. Arlene Litton.

"She's our horse trainer," Cooper explained, and he answered the call on speaker.

"Coop, we might have some trouble brewing," Arlene said. "I was out checking on some calves and spotted a car parked just on the other side of the east back fence. It's nestled in some trees, nearly out of sight. The engine's still warm and there's some fresh footprints leading from it and into the pasture. I wrote down the license plate number and called it in to Reed. He said he'd run it."

Jessa had no idea if this sort of thing happened often, but she was betting it didn't.

"What kind of car?" Cooper asked the woman.

"A black Jeep Cherokee."

Oh, mercy. That put her heart right in her throat, and she seriously doubted it was a coincidence that the vehicle matched the description of the one on the security footage from the lab.

Cooper got to his feet. "Look at the front fender," he instructed Arlene. "See anything?"

"Yeah." She must have picked up on the concern in Cooper's voice because it was now in hers. "It's bashed in real good, like he ran into something. What you want me to do about this, Coop?"

"Lock down the ranch and get some hands out to follow those tracks. I'll be right out to help. And, Arlene, be careful. This guy could be a killer, and we have to find him before he tries to come after Liam."

Chapter Eleven

Before Cooper even made it to the hall, Jessa caught up with him. "You're not really going out there, are you?"

Cooper nodded. "This guy isn't giving up, and he needs to be stopped." But he appreciated her concern. Not for himself, but for Liam. "I'll have Tucker stay here with you. Some of the other ranch hands, too. They'll surround the house and will have orders to shoot anyone who tries to get in."

Jessa opened her mouth as if ready to argue with that, but finally shook her head. "Just be careful."

Her concern took him back a bit, and he cursed that blasted kiss that had changed everything between them.

"You and Liam stay away from the windows," Cooper added, and he hurried out.

He didn't waste any time—he called Tucker and filled him in so his brother could start getting the ranch hands in place. Thankfully, Tucker was already inside. And Rayanne. Cooper didn't like the idea of relying on his surly sister for anything, but she was a deputy sheriff, and if it came down to it, she'd hopefully stop a killer from getting into the house.

Cooper hurried downstairs to his office and armed the security system, using the keypad by the front door. He'd be heading out soon, but before he did that he needed to check the cameras they had positioned throughout the property. He might get lucky and spot this guy.

Nothing was on the first camera in the part of the pasture where Arlene had spotted the Jeep. The camera angle was wrong for him to see the vehicle itself, but he had no doubt that it was there.

How far had the driver managed to get, and where the hell was he?

He saw some ranch hands on the second camera. They were hurrying toward the house. Good. As soon as they were in place, he'd be free to leave.

His father was on the third camera. Roy was also heading for the house, and he was armed with a rifle. Arlene, too. Even Seth was outside the guest cottage, and he was talking to one of the ranch hands, no doubt to find out what was going on.

But there was no sign of the man who'd driven that Jeep.

Cooper remembered the other attack at Donovan's. The guy had fired shots from the top floor and the roof there. He quickly panned the camera around as much as he could, and saw something that caused his stomach to clench.

There, on the roof of one of the barns, was a guy dressed in clothes that would have blended in with the other ranch hands—jeans, boots and a cowboy hat. The guy had a scope rifle next to him, but he didn't aim it at the house. Instead, the man aimed some kind of handheld device.

Cooper couldn't be positive, but judging from the way he was moving and adjusting it, the device was some kind of thermal-imaging equipment. If he was right, the idiot could use it to pinpoint not just how many people were inside the house but their exact locations. If he was looking for Jessa and Liam, he would have no trouble spotting them.

That got Cooper moving. He barreled up the stairs, taking them two at a time.

"Jessa?" he called out before he even reached the landing. He also fired off a text to Tucker so his brother would know the shooter's location. "Get Liam out of the room now!"

He figured that would scare her to death. It did. Jessa had no color in her face and was shaking from head to toe. But she had Liam sheltered in her arms when she came running out of the room toward him.

"Where's the gunman?" Jessa asked, her words running together.

"Too close. Come with me."

"My mother…"

"We'll let her know to hide, too."

Thankfully, Liam didn't seem to be aware of the immediate danger. He still had the toy horse and was wearing a cowboy hat that was many sizes too big for him. Later, Cooper would kick himself for allowing another attack like this to happen, but for now he just focused on getting them to safety.

The door to Rayanne's room flew open, and she came out, her gun aimed and ready. "What's going on?"

"There's a gunman on the roof of the barn nearest the house." He tipped his head in that direction. "Can you keep watch up here and make sure he doesn't come through the windows?"

She glanced at Liam. "He's after the boy?"

Cooper nodded and wanted to curse that he had to explain anything. If this were one of his brothers, there would have been no questions asked. "Yeah, he's after Liam," Cooper said.

Rayanne nodded. "If he comes through a window, how you want me to handle it?"

"Shoot to kill."

That she didn't question, but she did take out her phone. "I'm calling Rosalie to tell her to take cover."

"My mom, too," Jessa added. "They're in the kitchen together."

Rayanne just gave him a get-going gesture with her hand, made her phone call, and Cooper got Jessa moving again. When they reached the stairs, he spotted Tucker in the foyer, already standing guard by the front door.

"We're getting the hands out of the line of fire," Tucker relayed. "Away from the barn. If anyone tries to get in, the alarm will sound."

That was good, but the kidnapper didn't have to get inside to do some damage. He could start shooting through the walls.

"I'm taking Liam and Jessa to my office," Cooper said as they headed that way. It was on the opposite side of the house from the barn and the shooter. "Wait with them."

He'd been right about his brother not questioning anything. Well, not with words, anyway. He saw the hesitation in Tucker's eyes. Maybe because Tucker knew Cooper would hate to leave Liam. But he had no choice. It wasn't just his job to stop this shooter—it was what he needed to do to protect Liam.

With Tucker right behind them, Cooper led

Jessa to his office. Liam immediately spotted the framed photos and some books. "Wanna see," he said, and he wriggled to get down.

Jessa held on to him and went to the computer monitor, where Cooper still had the feed from the camera on the screen.

And Cooper's heart dropped again.

Jessa pointed to the screen. "Is that the barn roof where you saw the gunman?"

Yeah, and he was no longer there.

Cooper bit back the profanity that he was thinking and called Arlene. "This guy's on the move. He's wearing jeans, a dark blue shirt and a tan hat."

"I'll find him," Arlene promised, but he knew that was a promise she couldn't keep. He could be anywhere.

Cooper searched through all the cameras again. "I think he's got an infrared or thermal-imaging device. He'd aimed something at the house."

Jessa's eyes widened when she looked at Liam. "He'll know it's Liam because of his size."

"Yeah," Cooper settled for saying. He snared Tucker's gaze. "Go to the closet where Dad keeps his hunting equipment. There should be one of those silver Mylar blankets." It wasn't a perfect solution, but it would stop the majority of the body's heat loss, making it harder for the shooter to spot Jessa and Liam.

Tucker hurried off to get the blanket, and while Cooper kept watch on the computer screens, he maneuvered Jessa and Liam to the floor and beneath his desk.

"It's a game," Cooper said to Liam, hoping that he didn't sound as worried as he felt.

There were no toys in his office, but Cooper took off his badge and handed it to Liam. "Tank you," Liam babbled, and he smiled from ear to ear.

Jessa certainly wasn't smiling, probably because she knew the desk wouldn't stop bullets.

Cooper took the laptop to the floor with him so he could position himself in front of Jessa and Liam and watch the screen at the same time.

There was a lot of activity. Ranch hands were running around and getting into position, but there were still a lot of areas not covered. His dad was trying to do something about that. Seth, too. But it was a big ranch with plenty of barns, stables and outbuildings that a gunman could use—especially if the guy had been able to pinpoint their position.

"Here," Tucker said, hurrying back into the room.

He shook open the foil blanket and they put it

around Jessa and Liam. Of course, that wouldn't stop the shooter from using infrared to key in on Tucker and him, so Cooper took the laptop with him and they headed for the door.

"Make sure no one gets to them," he said to Tucker.

However, Cooper hadn't made it even a step when he heard a sound he darn sure didn't want to hear.

The security system.

It was just a pulsing beat. A warning that something or someone had triggered the alarm.

The gunman was in the house.

That sent Cooper right back to the security screen, and even though there weren't interior cameras, he could see a blinking light to indicate the point of entry. A window in the family room just off the kitchen.

Much too close.

Especially too close to Rosalie and Jessa's mom.

It didn't matter that the guy wasn't after them. This idiot might shoot them on sight to get to Liam. Hopefully, the women would both stay hidden, as Rayanne had told them to do.

He disarmed the security system to stop it before it went from a beep to a full blare. A noise like that would no doubt scare Liam and prevent

Cooper from hearing the gunman's movement in the house.

"Rayanne," Cooper called out. "We've got an intruder."

She didn't answer. Maybe because she couldn't hear him or had chosen not to hear. Or maybe she just didn't want to give her position away to a killer. Either way, Cooper couldn't count on her for help.

"Wait in here with Liam and Jessa," he said to Tucker, and Cooper ignored Jessa's whispered demands for him to stay put.

He peered out into the hall and didn't see anyone so he stepped out. Cooper motioned for Tucker to shut the door and lock it. His brother did, and Cooper went looking for the intruder.

There was no direct access to the family room from the left hall, so Cooper went to the right. Toward the front of the house and the stairs. If the Mylar blanket could fool the infrared device, then the guy might go to the guest rooms to look for Liam. At least that was where Cooper hoped he would go so he wouldn't be anywhere near Liam.

Cooper kept his gun ready, and he made a quick look around the corner and into the foyer.

No one.

However, he heard the footsteps. Slow and cautious on the stairs. Cooper pivoted in that direction, taking aim.

But it was only Rayanne.

She, too, had her gun ready. She didn't say a word, just lifted her eyebrow, but Cooper understood what she was asking.

Where was the intruder?

He tipped his head toward the other side of the stairs and in the direction where the security light had indicated the break-in.

Rayanne didn't make a sound, but some of the color drained from her face. Probably because she knew her sister was in that general area. It was too risky to call Rosalie and try to warn her—the gunman might be able to hear a phone ringing. Same with a text. If it made any kind of sound, it could be fatal for not just Rosalie but Linda, too, and whoever the heck else was in the kitchen.

Rayanne nodded, waited until Cooper started moving that way and followed along behind him. They inched their way toward the kitchen. No sound of footsteps, which could mean the guy was just lying in wait. If he was hell-bent on kidnapping Liam, then he might want to eliminate any obstacles first.

Cooper stopped when he reached the kitchen and looked around. Still no one. Not even Rosalie and Linda.

Where the heck were they?

He heard some movement in the sunroom, and both Rayanne and he took aim there.

"It's me," someone called out. Arlene. Cooper was about to tell her to get down, but she continued before he could say a word. "I think he's getting away." Arlene stepped into the doorway. "I heard him moving around in a couple of the rooms. Didn't want to shoot in case some of the hands were in there."

"Where'd the intruder go?" Cooper demanded, and he hurried to the family room where Arlene pointed.

"Stay here," Cooper told Arlene. "Rayanne, find your sister and Linda."

No one was in the family room, and he opened the door that led to the side yard. No sign of a runner. But he stepped outside, listening for any sound that would give away this idiot's position.

Nothing.

Cooper didn't want him in the house or even near it, but he sure as hell didn't want him getting away, either. He went to the side of the sunroom and looked around the corner.

And he cursed.

The kidnapper wasn't there, but he'd ditched his rifle and the thermal-imaging equipment, and he'd no doubt done that so he could escape fast. That didn't mean the guy wasn't armed, though. He probably had a handgun or two on him.

"Head there!" Cooper shouted out to several of the ranch hands. He pointed toward the pasture nearest the window.

Of course, the intruder had had precious seconds to use another way to escape. Or this could all be a ruse. The guy could be hiding, waiting for Cooper to go in pursuit, and then the bozo could use that opportunity to get back in the house.

"Any sign of him?" Arlene asked. She was in the doorway of the sunroom, her gaze firing all around, but she also had her phone sandwiched against her shoulder.

"Nothing. Where's Rosalie and Linda?"

"They're fine. They hid in the pantry."

Good. He hadn't wanted the intruder to take them as hostages. Or worse—harm them in some way.

"Who's on the phone?" Cooper asked Arlene while he kept watch.

She held up her hand in a wait-a-second gesture. "Yeah, I'll tell him." Arlene put away her phone and met Cooper's gaze for a split second. "That was Reed. He ran the license plate I called in. And he got a hit. The Jeep's registered to one of your suspects. Hector Dixon."

Chapter Twelve

Jessa prayed she wasn't making another mistake.

She'd already made so many by not keeping Liam safe, and she might be adding to that lack of safety. Ironic. Since she'd brought him to the Sweetwater Springs sheriff's office, a place where she shouldn't have to worry about repeat kidnapping attempts.

But then, she'd have to worry about that no matter where she was.

That was the reason she'd brought Liam with her when Cooper had said he was going to his office to question the suspects. She wanted a chance to confront Hector and demand that he explain why an armed intruder had used Hector's vehicle to drive to the ranch.

The front door of the office opened, and Jessa snapped in that direction, her body bracing itself for another attack. But it was only Tucker.

"Just checking on things," Tucker said. "Thought

you might like an extra hand." And he slid his hand over the gun in his holster.

Jessa was glad for the extra protection, even if it was Cooper's family.

"Don't worry," Cooper said to her. "Hector will be here soon."

Yes. Colt had called and insisted that he come in. Hector would be questioned, along with Donovan, who'd also been ordered back in for another round. There'd been no sign of Peggy, or they would have had all their suspects under the same roof.

That only made her stomach churn more.

Because Liam would be under that roof right along with them. Her mother and Rosalie had Liam in Cooper's office at the back of the building, and Jessa didn't think a hired gun would be stupid enough to come to the sheriff's office. But then, she'd thought the ranch was safe, too.

Cooper had already told her that she would be able to observe the interviews from the two-way mirror off the interview room. Jessa was past the observation stage. She wanted to question both of them, but Cooper hadn't budged on it. With reason. If either man said something that could lead to their arrest, Cooper didn't want that compromised by her being part of the interview.

Or maybe he was just worried she'd fly off the handle.

Jessa couldn't deny that it was a strong possibility.

Cooper got a paper cup of water from the cooler and handed it to her. "You could wait in my office with Liam," he reminded her—again.

"I want to see Hector when he walks through that door," she reminded him right back.

A heavy sigh left his mouth. "You've had a lot hit you today—"

"So have you." And he knew exactly what she meant. More than the attack, more than the hunt for the person responsible. They were both dealing with the results of the DNA test.

"I'll want the paternity test repeated, of course," she said, but her voice broke. The emotion flooded through her. She hadn't cried since the attack. Hadn't come close to falling apart. But Jessa felt as if that might happen now.

Cooper took hold of her arm as if he expected her to crumple into a heap. Probably because she looked on the verge of it. He led her out of the main squad room, past his office and to the break room.

"I'll have the test repeated," he assured her. "Do you really think I'd lie to you about something like that?"

No. But that was what tore at her even more.

He wouldn't lie, and that meant somehow she had to deal with a truth she wasn't sure she could face.

"I can't lose Liam." She'd been saying that a lot lately. Not just to Cooper but to herself. "And I'm not sure I can put this on the back burner while we try to catch this kidnapper."

Another sigh, and Cooper pulled her into his arms. She didn't want this. Okay, she did. But she didn't want to want it. She didn't want to want *him*.

"You can go ahead and cry if you think it'll help," he offered.

Just the offer was enough to make her want to choke back tears. She wasn't a crier by nature, and she'd been doing too much of it lately. Jessa stepped back from him. Not easily, though. Part of her wanted to stay in Cooper's arms and let him help her through this, but she knew that Cooper, and her reaction to him, was a huge part of the problem.

"We need to get answers from our suspects," she reminded him. Reminded herself, too. "Because everything points to someone trying to cover up an illegal adoption."

"Yeah," he said. "There are some open cases on missing babies. Our situation might be connected to those."

Jessa thought about that a moment and didn't

like any of the conclusions she reached. Judging from the way Cooper's forehead bunched up, neither did he. It was especially troubling that his wife could have been murdered so that someone—a monster—could take Liam.

There was a knock at the door just a split second before it opened. It was Colt. Even though Jessa was no longer in Cooper's arms, she stepped back farther to put more distance between them. That only made Colt give his brother a suspicious glance. She figured Colt wasn't stupid, and he could see the attraction between Cooper and her.

"I got the financials and background checks on Hector and Peggy," Colt said, handing Cooper a half-inch-thick file. "There's plenty to read in them, but some highlights—there are some suspicious deposits in Peggy's account. By suspicious, I mean two or three times a month, she makes cash deposits of anywhere from five to ten grand."

"Money she's getting from being a baby broker," Cooper supplied. "Do the deposits line up with the dates of the adoptions?"

"Hard to tell. Those records she left Jessa are a mess, and we're still trying to untangle them." He paused. "Our FBI *stepbrother* offered to help."

Cooper pulled back his shoulders. For a second, anyway. "Let him help. If he thinks he can make sense of it, let him try."

"He's not doing this for us," Colt reminded him. "But because he wants to help Rosalie find her missing daughter."

Cooper nodded. "I don't care why he's doing it. We just need to get to the truth." He thumbed through the file, and she saw something highlighted that had caught Cooper's attention.

"Two days ago Hector made a payment to Vernon Graham," Jessa said, moving closer so she could get a better look.

"Well, Hector didn't make the payment directly," Colt explained. "It came out of his business expenses. His assistant actually signed the check."

The amount was only a hundred dollars. Not exactly enough for a hired gun. Still, it was a direct connection between Hector and Graham.

Or was it?

Her attention landed on another highlight on the next page. A payment that Peggy had made to Graham for the same amount—a hundred dollars, and the check had been made out on the same day as Hector's payment.

Cooper shook his head. "This is starting to look like a setup."

"I agree," Colt said, "But it could be a reverse psychology. If all our suspects look guilty, then we don't know which one to arrest."

"Yeah." Cooper looked up from the papers. "Make that call to Seth and ask for his help."

Colt hesitantly nodded and turned, no doubt ready to make what Cooper would see as an unholy alliance with their stepbrother. However, he stopped when the front door opened.

"I'll call Seth in a few minutes. Right now, it's showtime," Colt said. "Hector Dixon's here."

Even though Cooper tried to stay ahead of her, Jessa didn't let him. She hurried past Colt and practically ran to the reception area. And Hector was indeed there.

His gaze narrowed immediately when he saw her. "This is your doing—again. I'm fed up with you and the sheriff accusing me of wrongdoing."

"Someone tried to kidnap Liam again," Jessa settled for saying, though she wanted to say plenty more to him. Actually, she wanted to make him tell her the truth, and it sickened her a little that she was ready to use force to do that.

Her news softened Hector's glare, but she couldn't be sure if his reaction was because he genuinely felt sorry for her or because he was faking it to take suspicion off himself.

"This way," Cooper insisted, tipping his head to one of the interview rooms. He picked up a laptop, some files, and led Hector inside. Once there, Cooper met his brother's gaze, and Tucker took Jessa into the observation room so she could watch.

"I know about the DNA test," Tucker said the moment his brother was out of earshot. "I talked to Doc Howland about it to make sure there was no chance it was wrong. He's positive that Liam is indeed Cooper's son."

Oh, God. If the doctor had talked to Tucker about it, that meant soon it could be all over town. Everyone would know, and all those people would be telling Cooper how happy they were for him. His family would no doubt be pressing for him to claim Liam and kick her out of the picture.

"The doc was worried about Cooper," Tucker went on. "About you, too. And he wanted me to make sure you were both okay."

"We're not okay," Jessa said under her breath.

Tucker just stared at her. No sympathy. No assurance that all would be well.

He looked a lot like Cooper. Same gray eyes. Same dark hair. But Jessa knew Tucker had a reputation for being a ladies' man. And a reputation for bending the law. He would do anything it took to make sure she didn't stand in the way of Cooper getting his son back.

"Cooper nearly died when he lost them," Tucker continued. He didn't look at her now. Instead, he fastened his gaze to his brother on the other side of the glass. "He won't go through another ordeal like that."

But Jessa certainly would, and it broke her heart to think of just how quickly she could lose the child she'd raised. It made her want to snatch up Liam and run. Anywhere. Anyplace where Cooper couldn't claim him. However, she could be running straight into the arms of a kidnapper.

Or worse.

It'd occurred to her that the person trying to cover up the kidnapping might be willing to do anything to make sure Liam couldn't be linked back to him.

Anything.

Tucker cursed, caught her arm and put her in the only chair in the room. "Are you about to faint?" he snarled.

She must have looked pretty bad for him to think that, and Tucker seemed as uncomfortable playing nursemaid to her as she was to be on the receiving end of it.

"Just breathe," he grumbled.

She couldn't do that well, either. But she did watch Cooper, and she prayed he'd get a break in the case to end the danger.

Then she could think of running with Liam.

Cooper took a piece of paper from the file Colt had given him and he slid it Hector's way. "That's the registration for your Jeep Cherokee. A man used it to drive to my family's ranch. He broke in, and I believe he tried to kidnap Liam."

Hector started shaking his head before Cooper even finished. "I keep that vehicle out at my hunting cabin. Anyone could have borrowed it to set me up for this."

He hadn't hesitated on the answer. Maybe because he'd been expecting the question. Still, it seemed risky for Hector's hired gun to use a vehicle registered to him. But again, Hector could have done that, hoping it would smack of a setup.

Cooper looked through the rest of the papers. "I don't see a hunting cabin listed in your assets, but there's one in your sister's name."

"It belongs to both of us, but her name is on the deed. We don't use the place very often. That's why I wouldn't have noticed the Jeep was missing."

"I'll send the Rangers out to the cabin." Cooper glanced back in Tucker's direction, and his brother made the call to get that started. "If the Jeep is there, they'll process it for any evidence." Cooper went to the next page. "Do you know Vernon Graham?"

"I know of him. He's one of the men who tried to kidnap Liam. Last I heard, he was in the hospital."

"You never had any dealings with him?"

"None," Hector insisted.

Which meant he'd just lied.

Cooper slid another piece of paper Hector's way. "Then why did you pay Vernon Graham a hundred dollars?"

Hector looked at the transaction as if seeing it for the first time. "I didn't pay him. But my assistant often gives contributions to various charities in my name."

It was either a very convenient answer or Hector had messed up and left a paper trail connecting him to a man he'd hired to kidnap a little boy.

Hector opened his mouth to say something else, but his phone rang. "I'll turn it off," he mumbled, but then seemed to freeze when he looked at the screen. "I think the caller might be Peggy."

That got Cooper's attention. He took the phone from Hector and answered it on speaker.

"Hector?" the caller immediately said. "Where are you?"

It was Peggy, all right, and Tucker hurried from the room, no doubt so he could try to trace the call. Jessa didn't stay put, either. She went to the interview room and threw open the door. Hector spared her a glance. A nasty one. Before he turned his attention back to Peggy.

"I'm at the sheriff's office *again,*" Hector answered.

"Don't hang up," Cooper warned the woman. "Tell me where you are."

Peggy didn't jump to answer, and Jessa prayed she'd stay on the line until Colt and Tucker had a chance to pinpoint her location. "I'm someplace safe, I hope. I know you don't believe me, but someone's trying to kill me."

"I might believe you if you turned yourself in. You held a man and two women at gunpoint. You need to answer for that."

"And I will. When you have this would-be killer behind bars so he can't get to me." She paused. "But I might have been wrong about Donovan. He might not be behind the illegal adoptions."

"You seemed pretty sure he was guilty when you were holding him hostage," Cooper reminded her.

"Yes, but I think Hector could have misled me so he could cover up his own guilt."

"Right," Hector snarled. "Point at me now, will you? Well, I'm not the one who did something wrong. Hell, Peggy…" He stopped, obviously struggling to keep a leash on his temper. "Quit slinging mud at me so we can get to the bottom of this. Someone tried to kidnap Jessa's boy again."

Peggy made a sound. Hard to interpret what it meant, though. "I didn't know."

"Well, you do now," Cooper snapped. He

grabbed one of the papers from the file. "Now tell me about these deposits made to your bank account." He started reading off the sums and the dates.

"I told you. People pay me to find the perfect match for the babies."

"But I wasn't perfect," Jessa said. "I was single."

"The *perfect match* for someone who can afford it," Peggy corrected in a very loud voice. "You paid for your son, and it's payments like yours that keep the adoption wheels turning. If I had to work elsewhere in a day job, I wouldn't have time to find babies in need of adoption."

Then people would have to go through normal channels. Channels that Jessa hadn't taken because it would have been years, if ever, before she'd gotten a child. It sickened her though to think that cutting corners had brought them to this point. Not just her, but countless others.

"Did you steal Liam?" Cooper came right out and asked.

"No." Peggy didn't raise her voice. She merely sighed and then hung up.

Cooper hit Redial and stuck his head out into the hall. "Did you get her location?"

"Sorry," Tucker said a moment later. "It's a burner."

Cooper and Jessa both groaned, and he added

some profanity when the woman didn't answer. A burner was a prepaid cell that couldn't be traced. However, that did cause Jessa to snap in Hector's direction.

"How did you know it was Peggy who was calling?" Jessa demanded.

He lifted his shoulder. "Peggy's called me before, and it's appeared on the screen as unknown name, unknown number."

"It's how she called me," someone said. Jessa hadn't heard him come up the hall, but it was Donovan. And he wasn't alone. There were two men wearing suits standing behind him. His lawyers, no doubt.

"You're going in there," Cooper ordered Donovan, and he pointed to the interview room across the hall.

Donovan walked closer, that oily smile on his mouth. She figured that smile got to Cooper, because it sure as heck got to her. There was nothing about this situation that warranted a smile.

"Cooper," Donovan said, his tone as condescending as that smile. "I know you'd love to see me suffer. But this vendetta against me has got to stop. In fact, my lawyers are here to tell you that there'll be no more questions…unless you file charges against me."

Jessa knew Cooper couldn't do that. Not yet, anyway. The only evidence they had against

Donovan was Peggy's accusations, and considering Peggy's situation, those weren't nearly enough to bring charges against the man.

"Now, if you don't mind," Donovan said, casually checking the time on his pricey watch, "I'll just be going. I have a business to run."

Donovan turned as if ready to leave, but he stopped and looked at Hector, who was still in the interview room. "Don't I know you from somewhere?"

Hector shook his head. Maybe too quickly.

"Funny," Donovan remarked. "I could have sworn I've seen you around Sweetwater Springs."

With that, Donovan smiled again and strolled away. Jessa sure didn't smile, and neither did Cooper. They just stared at Hector, waiting to see if Donovan had hit a nerve or was just blowing smoke.

"I was here in town after the flood," Hector finally said.

He didn't have to clarify what flood. Jessa knew from Cooper's suddenly blanched expression that Hector was talking about the one that had swept away his wife.

"A former client lives here," Hector went on, "and she had some flood damage. Not Donovan, but a rancher just outside of town. Norma Cullen."

Jessa knew the name, had seen it on records

for an old embezzlement case, but she'd never met the woman.

"Norma asked me to come out and take a look at the damage," Hector went on. "I don't normally handle that sort of thing, but I made an exception because she was an old high school friend."

"That's all there was to the visit?" Cooper said, and it sounded like some kind of accusation.

"That's all," Hector snapped. "I don't know how Donovan found out about me being in town, and the only reason he brought it up was to implicate me in all of this."

"You're already implicated," Cooper reminded him. He opened a file on the laptop. A file with photos of a white car and another of Molly. "Did you see my wife, that car, the baby, anything?"

Hector studied the photos and shook his head to each of the questions. "Donovan's just muddying the waters. And now, if you'll excuse me— and even if you don't—I think I'll take a page from Donovan's book and leave. When and if you have more than just speculation, contact me."

"Oh, I will. Maybe as soon as the crime scene folks find something in that Jeep that will lead right back to you."

Hector stopped, stiffened. "If you find anything, it's because someone planted it." He walked out. Or rather, stormed out, slamming the door behind him.

Cooper stood there, staring after the man's hasty exit. But he didn't stand there alone for long. Colt went to one side of him. Tucker, the other. A united front. A family. Even with the shadow hanging over them from Jewell's trial, they were still very much a family.

One that would make sure Cooper got his son back.

Jessa got that urge again. To grab Liam and run. But then Cooper looked over his shoulder at her.

"I'm sorry," he said, his voice far more soothing than it should have been. He walked closer to her. "I wanted to get more out of them."

And he surprised her—surprised his brothers, too—by brushing a kiss on her mouth. It was quick. Barely a kiss. But she felt it all the way to her toes. Colt and Tucker no doubt felt something entirely different.

Confusion.

They probably thought Cooper had lost his mind.

"Come on," Cooper said to her, ignoring his brothers' stares. "We'll get Liam back to the ranch." He put his hand on the small of her back, easing her in that direction.

But he stopped.

Jessa followed his gaze to the glass front door and the woman who stepped inside. Rosalie.

"We need to talk," Rosalie said, not to her brothers but to Jessa.

She didn't like the sound of gloom and doom in Rosalie's voice. There'd already been way too much bad news. Jessa couldn't handle more.

"You remember I told you I'd been investigating missing babies? Like my own daughter," Rosalie explained.

Not trusting her voice, Jessa just nodded.

"Well, I found out something," Cooper's sister continued. "About Liam."

Chapter Thirteen

Cooper just stood there, staring at his sister. He tried to tamp down his hopes. But it was hard to do that when Rosalie might have exactly what he needed to put an end to the danger.

And reclaim his son.

Of course, he couldn't do that without hurting Jessa. Maybe Liam, too. After all, Jessa was the only parent Liam remembered having. Still, that didn't mean Cooper would just hand him over to her and bow out of Liam's life.

However, that left him with one Texas-size question: What was he going to do?

"What did you find out?" Jessa asked Rosalie.

Jessa was definitely wearing her heart on her sleeve. Her voice was mostly breath. She was pale and shaky. And she, too, looked as if she were trying to tamp down something—a panic attack, maybe.

Rosalie took a moment to gather her breath. "I've been working with criminal informants and just about anyone else who could give me information about my missing daughter."

Cooper almost gave her a stern scolding for that. It was dangerous, and she should leave that sort of thing to the cops. Still, he knew what Rosalie was going through, and he would have bargained with the devil himself to get his son back. Rosalie no doubt felt the same way about her own child.

"One of the informants told me about a woman who found a baby," Rosalie continued. "The timing and circumstances are right for it to have been Liam."

"But you're not sure," Jessa jumped to say.

There was sympathy in Rosalie's eyes, and she volleyed glances between Jessa and Cooper as if asking if she should continue. Cooper just nodded.

Rosalie took another deep breath. "The woman refuses to talk to me, and the informant wouldn't give me her name even when I offered him money."

"If you think he's telling the truth, I'll offer him enough money so he'll talk," Cooper assured her. "What's his name?"

"Calvin Brinton. He lives in San Antonio. And he has a record a mile long, mainly for petty stuff, but he did some time for forgery about a decade ago."

Cooper looked at Colt. "I'm on it," Colt assured

him, and he hurried back to one of the offices, no doubt to make a call to locate everything he could about this criminal informant.

"Brinton said a woman who was a friend of friend had found a baby boy nearly two years ago after the flood," Rosalie continued. "According to this woman, the baby was floating in his car seat, and she rescued him."

God, it was hard to hear this. His son could have been out there on that raging creek. A dozen bad things could have happened to him. If this woman was telling the truth about rescuing him, then she had also saved his life.

Jessa started shaking her head. "Why didn't the woman report it?"

Cooper had the same damn question. He'd died a thousand times after Molly's death and his son's disappearance. And yeah, he was thankful for the rescue, but not thankful that his baby had been kept from him.

"This is where the story gets a little sticky," Rosalie went on. "The woman says she'd heard of someone who would pay big bucks for a healthy newborn, so she made some calls and arranged to meet with this person."

That immediately got his attention. "Peggy Dawes?"

"No. I'm sorry." She turned to Jessa. "She said the woman was *you*."

"Then she's lying," Jessa insisted. "She's lying," she repeated to Cooper.

He ignored her for the time being. "What else did the woman tell your criminal informant?"

Rosalie didn't look especially eager to continue, but she nodded eventually. "She said that Jessa wanted the adoption to look aboveboard, so she gave the woman the name of a baby broker who was in turn supposed to contact an adoption attorney."

"I didn't," Jessa protested. She caught Cooper's arms, pulling him around to face her. "I wouldn't do anything like that."

"I know. But we could still get some truthful information from this woman if we can find her. My guess is that she's covering for the real kidnapper and purposely gave that false info about you to the criminal informant."

Jessa stayed quiet a moment, obviously giving that some thought, and he saw the muscles in her arms and shoulders relax a bit when she realized he wasn't accusing her of anything.

"We need to start by locating the criminal informant and pressuring him to give us her name," Cooper said, and he met Rosalie's gaze. "Thank you for bringing this to me."

Rosalie nodded, but she didn't get a chance to say anything because Tucker spoke first.

"Who else knows about this Calvin Brinton

and what he told you?" he asked Rosalie. Unlike Cooper, Tucker's question sounded more like an interrogation.

Rosalie lifted her shoulder. "I'm not sure. I've talked to a lot of people, and Brinton's someone I use often when I'm following a lead."

Cooper and Tucker exchanged glances, and Cooper knew what had triggered his brother's question.

Hell.

"This could put both Brinton and you in danger," Cooper told his sister. "The woman, too. Until we get this situation under control, it's best if you take some precautions. Don't go anywhere unless one of us or your sister is with you."

Cooper had expected that to frighten Rosalie, but it didn't. She only gave a resolute nod. He wanted to add that she should back off from her investigation for a while, but a mere request from him wouldn't stop a parent in search of her missing child. Heck, once the danger was over for Liam and Jessa, Cooper would jump to help Rosalie himself.

Tucker mumbled plenty of profanity. Maybe because he didn't like being joined at the hip with a sister they no longer considered a sister. At least that had been the case when Rosalie had first shown up at the ranch with Jewell's entourage. However, Rosalie had more than pulled her own weight by helping to take care of Liam. And now she'd given them a lead.

Maybe.

If it wasn't already too late.

One glance at Tucker and Cooper realized his brother was thinking the same thing.

Tucker took out his phone. "I'll find out if there are any missing persons reports or dead bodies that might match this woman who found the baby."

"But you don't know anything about her," Rosalie interrupted.

"She must live near the creek," Cooper explained while Tucker proceeded with the call. "And she's probably not elderly if she walked down to the creek so soon after the flood. Also, since she was willing to commit a crime by selling the baby, then she possibly has a criminal record."

Of course, it still could turn out to be a needle in a haystack, but it was a start.

Jessa went closer to him. "I know I sound like Hector, Peggy and Donovan, but I didn't do anything wrong."

"I know." And Cooper would have given her more reassurance than that if Colt hadn't finished his call.

"It's not good," Colt told them right off the bat. "I just spoke to a friend in San Antonio P.D., and

Calvin Brinton was found dead just a few hours ago. Murdered, execution-style."

Rosalie's hand flew to her mouth, but Cooper could still see her lips trembling. Jessa wasn't faring much better. Maybe because she was thinking this would implicate her in a murder, but in Cooper's book, it didn't.

"It's not your fault," Cooper immediately said to Rosalie. "I wouldn't be surprised if the person behind these attacks paid Brinton to contact you just so he could implicate Jessa."

Jessa nodded, but she lost more of the color on her cheeks. "He wants us divided. He wants me to take Liam and run. That way I'll be an easier target."

Cooper nodded, too. "I figure this guy will do anything to eliminate any chance that Liam could be linked back to him."

There'd already been a lot of effort made to cover up that link. The kidnapping attempts. The break-in at the lab to destroy the DNA sample. Now Brinton's murder.

Colt finished another call and joined them. "I've put out feelers. Whoever this woman is, we'll find her. Hopefully alive," he added in a mumble.

"Come on," Cooper said to Jessa. "We should get Liam back to the ranch. Rosalie, too."

"Wait. What are you gonna do?" Tucker asked

with his hands on his hips and his gaze firmly planted on Cooper.

He didn't think Tucker was talking about the danger now. "I'll have to sort it out with Jessa," Cooper settled for saying.

That caused Tucker to huff. "For Pete's sake, Liam's your son, and you've already lost too much time with him."

Colt made a sound of agreement. "All you have to do is show any judge those DNA results, and that'll start the process to revoke the adoption."

Cooper couldn't deny what his brothers were saying. Neither could Jessa. If he pushed, he could have custody of Liam by the end of the month. No matter which way he went with this, it would mean a drastic change in all their lives.

"Well?" Tucker prompted. "Please tell me you aren't just gonna let her take him."

"No." Cooper's gaze came to hers. "I'm going to do what's best for Liam. I'm having Jessa and him move to the ranch and live with me."

Chapter Fourteen

Jessa paced outside Cooper's office while she waited for him to finish the family meeting with his father and brothers. There wasn't much else she could do—especially since Cooper hadn't invited her to join in on the discussion.

Liam had been bathed, fed and was down for the night. Her mother had said good-night, too. The ranch house was quiet, well guarded, and Jessa should be trying to settle herself so she could get some rest.

Fat chance of that, though.

She wasn't resting until she had a chance to confront Cooper about his idiotic insistence that she move to the ranch. He certainly hadn't made it sound like an invitation. More like one of his orders. And yes, their relationship had gotten a little friendlier.

All right, a *lot* friendlier.

However, that didn't mean it was a good idea for them to be under the same roof for an extended period of time. It would only make things harder for her to distance herself from him. And distance him from Liam.

As if she could.

No, Cooper wouldn't just let Liam go, but she had to find a way to minimize the damage and guard her heart in the process.

The sound of voices snagged her attention again. Jessa could hear parts of the conversation from the four McKinnon men. Some parts were easier to hear than others because the meeting involved some raised voices. Apparently, she wasn't the only one who thought the moving-in order was a bad idea. Tucker was especially against it.

No surprise there.

Like Cooper, Tucker had been especially critical of her pressing for Jewell's arrest. And like Cooper, his criticism hadn't been because he wanted to defend Jewell but because he saw the investigation as a threat to the rest of his family. Especially his father.

However, his father didn't agree with Tucker on the matter of Cooper's order. Roy was all for the idea of Liam and her moving to the ranch. Permanently.

She heard a phone ring. A moment later, the door flew open and Tucker stormed out. Not before giving her a glare that could have withered every blade of grass in Texas. Jessa fared somewhat better from Roy. He whispered an apology—for what, he didn't say—and walked away.

Colt was on the phone and didn't even make eye contact with her when he came out. Still, she was pretty certain they blamed her for this. They probably thought she'd managed to talk Cooper into this stupid moving-in-with-them idea.

She didn't wait for an invitation from Cooper. Jessa went inside the office and immediately spotted the baby monitor on his desk. It was on, and she could see her son sleeping peacefully in the crib. She was pleased about that but not pleased that Cooper was already acting like a parent.

Jessa mentally groaned. Of course he would think that he had a right to act that way. And he did. But she hated that there was nothing she could do to stop him from chipping away at her claim on the child she'd raised.

There was more proof of that on the desk.

The DNA results that proved Liam was Cooper's son. Not some handwritten note, but the actual lab report. She'd used reports just like that to prove a case in court.

Cooper would no doubt use it for the same reason.

"Doc Howland sent it over," Cooper explained. "He's keeping it under wraps for now. And since he didn't want anything on file, that's the only copy."

Cooper's eyes met hers. For an instant she saw the bone-weary fatigue there. However, he must have seen the fight in hers, because he frowned and mumbled some profanity under his breath.

"Why ask me to move in with you?" she demanded, and didn't wait for his answer. "Did you think it was the fastest way to get custody of Liam?"

"No. I thought it was what I should do for Liam. And for you." Cooper scrubbed his hand over his face, walked closer.

That threw her for a moment. Jessa had braced herself for the kind of stubborn, riled attitude she'd gotten from Tucker. But Cooper just seemed as exhausted as she was.

"I love Liam," Cooper went on. "And it wouldn't do anyone any good to push you out of his life. It sure wouldn't be in his best interest."

"It wouldn't do anyone any good except for you," Jessa corrected.

"Yeah. I'd have my boy to myself, but it'd come at a high cost." He paused, glanced at the photo of his wife on his desk next to the baby monitor. "Liam doesn't remember Molly, but he sure as heck knows you. It wouldn't be fair to cut you out of his life."

Jessa hadn't braced herself for a lot of things,

including fairness. It softened her anger a lot more than she wanted it to.

"But moving in here at the ranch?" she questioned. "You can't think that's a good idea."

He lifted his shoulder. "We could make it work."

"Really? For one thing, your family wouldn't like that." Then she pointed to Molly's photo. "And you're still in love with your late wife."

Cooper didn't deny either accusation, but he did take the photo, and after a long look, he eased it into his desk drawer and shut it.

Jessa sighed. "I didn't say that to make you put the photo away. I'd hoped it would make you see that we're not suited for living with each other."

His eyebrow lifted. "Really?" he repeated.

She felt the heat rise on her cheeks. And elsewhere. With just one word Cooper could remind her of that mistake of a kissing session. Except it hadn't felt like a mistake at the time.

Sadly, it still didn't.

And that was why it was indeed a mistake.

"We're attracted to each other," he pointed out.

"Attraction's not enough," she insisted. Though there were times, like now, when it certainly felt as if it could help them overcome a lot of things.

"We're both committed to Liam," he said, coming toward her. Cooper stopped just inches from her. The weariness vanished from his eyes, and he pointed his finger at her. "And if you repeat that part about attraction not being enough, I'll remind you otherwise."

Jessa swallowed hard. She was all too familiar with Cooper's reminders. The kisses. The smoldering looks. Her body being in a continuous state of arousal just by being around him.

"Being committed to Liam and this attraction aren't enough," she reminded him.

"It's a start," he reminded her right back.

Okay. She was clearly losing this argument, and it was one she couldn't afford to lose.

Could she?

Would it really be that bad if she gave in to his order?

For just a moment Jessa allowed herself to think about living with Cooper. Not just for the immediate future until the danger had passed. But, well, forever. It would have some advantages. Like no messy custody dispute over Liam.

And maybe even sharing a bed with Cooper.

She couldn't stop that from creeping into her mind. However, she still shook her head. She didn't say a word, but her answer to the ridiculous living arrangements must have been all over her face, because Cooper hooked his arm around to snap her to him.

And he kissed her.

Jessa put her hands against his chest to push

him away. At least some small part of her wanted to do that, but the other parts won out, and she found herself falling deeper into his arms.

All in all, not a bad place to be.

With her body pressed against his, and his mouth moving over hers as if he knew exactly how to set her on fire.

Jessa tried to hang on, tried to voice some kind of reminder that this wasn't going to help their situation. It would only muddy already muddy waters. But did she say that?

No.

She just stayed put in his arms and returned the kiss. Boy, did she. Jessa was the one who deepened it, and she was the one who tugged Cooper closer and closer until they were plastered against each other.

Until she was burning for him.

Soon, very soon, all thoughts of Cooper's order for her to move to the ranch slipped from her mind. Common sense did, too. She wanted to blame it all on the fact that it'd been so long since she'd been kissed like this. So long since she'd been held and wanted. But this wasn't about time.

This was all Cooper's doing. And she was terrified that even if this continued, it wouldn't leave her satisfied for long, that she would only end up wanting him more.

Cooper reached behind him and locked the

door. She realized then what he had in mind. To take this much further than a scalding-hot kissing session.

That still didn't stop her.

Since this was going to be a massive mistake, Jessa figured she might as well enjoy it.

And pay the price for it later.

COOPER DIDN'T QUESTION what he was doing. He just went with it. He pushed aside the investigation, the looming custody fight. Even his insistence that Jessa move in with him.

And he just let himself get lost in her.

It wasn't hard to do. She tasted like Christmas and all the other good things rolled into one. Felt that way, too. With her breasts against his chest. Cooper did something to make the pressure even better—and worse—by catching the back of her leg and lifting it so that her sex met his.

Damn good.

And once he got his eyes uncrossed he did something about ridding her of some of the blasted clothes between them.

Jessa was doing some clothes removal of her own. Not easily. She stayed with the kissing until she was out of breath and gasping. She broke away only long enough to pull some air into her lungs and then continued unbuttoning his shirt. She finally managed to get it off him.

Her touch was instant. Her fingers against his bare skin created some instant heat inside him. Not that he needed more. He was already crazy enough, but it sped things up for Cooper, and he rid Jessa of her top. Then her bra. She was small, firm. Perfect.

Tasted perfect, too, he discovered when he lowered his head and kissed her there.

Jessa reacted. Man, did she. She made a little sound of pleasure and pulled him closer for even more. That sent him fumbling to get them to the sofa. He darn sure didn't want to wait to take her upstairs. Everything inside him was yelling for him to take her *now*.

But something else yelled through his brain.

"I don't have a condom," he let her know. Not easily. He damn sure didn't want this to end.

With her breath still gusting and her fingers on his zipper, Jessa froze. Met his gaze. She seemed to have a split-second debate with herself and yanked him back to her for another kiss.

"I'm on the pill," she said through the frantic flurry of kisses she showered on his face.

That was the best news he'd heard in a long time. Cooper knew he should still back off, but he would have had a better chance of telling his heart to stop beating. This was going to happen even if it didn't make sense.

Jessa obviously felt the same way.

She went after his zipper again. He went after hers.

They weren't exactly graceful when they landed on the sofa. That gracefulness went down another significant notch when she worked her hand into his boxers and took hold of him.

Oh, man. He was in big trouble here.

Her touch made everything seem more urgent, and Cooper rid her of her jeans. Panties, too. And even though he was burning, he still took the time to look at her.

And taste her.

Yeah, she was perfect everywhere.

Jessa made more of those sounds of pleasure. Slow, silky moans that purred from her throat. But there was nothing slow about her touch. She was frantic when she pushed off his boots and jeans, and by the time she made it to his boxers, she was well past the frantic stage.

Cooper was right there with her.

As soon as he was free of his boxers, he caught her and sank deep and hard into her. The pleasure shot through him, robbing him of his breath. He wanted to savor this, too, as he'd done with the sight of her. But Jessa lifted her hips, and savoring was a lost cause.

Cooper moved inside her and Jessa moved with

him, keeping up the already desperate pace. That pace would end all of this too soon, but there was nothing he could do to make their bodies slow down. That fierce need pushed them hard to complete this and find mind-numbing release.

Too bad that release wouldn't last long. But Cooper refused to deal with that now. He only dealt with Jessa, and the frenzied rhythm of the strokes inside her.

"Finish this," she whispered. "Finish *me*."

That was the plan. Cooper pushed into her, felt her body give way to the maddening strokes. He felt her *finish*. But she didn't go alone. Nope. Jessa hooked her arm around his back and pulled him down for a kiss.

That was the last straw for him.

Cooper buried his face against her neck and let Jessa finish him off.

Yeah, he'd been right about the mind-numbing part. Right about a lot of other things, too.

Now all that was left was dealing with the aftermath of the mistake he'd just made.

Chapter Fifteen

Jessa felt the instant change in Cooper. The muscles in his back tightened, and while he couldn't exactly roll off her without landing on the floor, he did move to his side.

He didn't say a word. Didn't need to. She could also feel the fierce debate going on inside him.

Because she was having the same debate with herself.

For days they'd been skirting around this heated attraction, and her body welcomed the satisfaction. The release. But she figured it would come at a high price, and she didn't want Cooper— or herself—making assumptions that this meant anything. Anything other than great sex, that was.

It'd been so long since she'd been with a man. And never like this. Why the heck had he been just as good as he looked?

Jessa mentally sighed. It would have been so much easier if she just felt indifferent toward

Cooper. Or if she'd just left him alone. After all, this was the man who could destroy her life, and here she'd landed in bed with him.

Well, on the sofa, anyway.

"This doesn't mean I'll move in with you," she let him know.

He lifted one eyelid, and it looked as if he tried to glare at her. Hard to do that, though, while butt naked and squished on a sofa together. "Didn't figure it did."

Her feelings were all over the place, and while his words were right, they didn't make her feel so right. Because if he hadn't used sex to sway her into moving in with him, then that meant this attraction had just gotten the better of both of them. It also meant the attraction would only get worse.

Until it burned itself out.

Then what?

They'd be at odds under the same roof. Maybe Cooper couldn't see the problem with that now, but he would certainly see it later. And being at odds with her might prompt him to get her off the ranch.

Without Liam, of course.

There was no way Cooper would let her leave with Liam now that he knew the little boy was his son.

"Don't know if you know this, but your nostrils

flare when you're getting upset," he drawled. "So other than the obvious, what's upsetting you?"

She wanted to bring up the argument that she'd just mentally had with herself, but one look at him and Jessa knew he was well aware of what she'd been thinking.

"Just the obvious," she settled for saying.

Cooper made a sound of agreement and glanced at the baby monitor, prompting her to do the same. Thankfully, Liam was sleeping just as he should be. And it was a reminder she should be upstairs with him.

Jessa moved, forcing herself to get up, and she wished the room was suddenly pitch-black so that Cooper couldn't see her naked. He seemed to have no such concerns. He stood right in front of her.

Mercy.

The man had a great body.

Perfect. All those toned muscles earned from hard work on the ranch. The rugged face. It didn't help that she still had the taste of him on her lips.

And just like that, she felt herself go all warm again. A warmth that Jessa tried to push away so she could gather up her clothes and get dressed.

"How bad are you regretting this?" he asked just as he zipped up his jeans.

"Not bad enough." Especially considering that she was still fantasizing about getting him back on the sofa with her at the same time that she was worrying about his claim on Liam.

Cooper chuckled. Leaned over and kissed her. Not a postsex kind of peck, either. It was a full kiss that reminded her that one round of sex wasn't going to rid her of this sudden need she had for Cooper.

"How bad are you regretting this?" she asked, throwing the question back at him.

He pushed her hair from her face. Dropped another kiss on her forehead. Then met her eye to eye. Jessa was instantly sorry that she'd opened herself up for this conversation, because the last thing she wanted to hear was Cooper say he would do whatever it took to get custody of Liam.

Even though that was exactly what he would do.

And she would fight him equally hard.

"Let's table that for now," he said just as his phone buzzed.

Jessa thought maybe she'd like to table that particular discussion for a lifetime and have things go on as they had been.

Well, minus the danger, of course.

And when she saw Colt's name on Cooper's phone screen, it was a stark reminder of not just the investigation but the danger that had set all this in motion.

"I found something," Colt said the moment

Cooper answered the call and put it on speaker. "I'm pretty sure I found the woman who talked to Rosalie's criminal informant. Sonya Eakins."

Cooper shook his head. "I don't know her." And he looked back at Jessa, who had to shake her head, too. She quickly started dressing in case they had to go to the sheriff's office to question this woman.

"She lived in a little place just a quarter of a mile from the creek," Colt added.

Jessa didn't miss Colt's use of the past tense. "Sonya Eakins is dead?"

"Yeah," Colt verified. "SAPD found her body this morning. Killed execution-style."

Sweet heaven. This just kept getting worse.

Cooper cursed. "You're sure she's the right woman?" he asked his brother.

"Pretty sure. Everything you said about her fits. About six months before the flood, she rented the house within walking distance of the creek. She was young, early thirties, and had a long rap sheet for embezzlement and theft."

And to think Liam could have been in this woman's hands. At least Sonya hadn't hurt him, probably because she'd seen him as goods to sell.

"I got access to Sonya's bank accounts," Colt continued, "and there was a five-thousand-dollar deposit made less than a week after the flood."

Well, it wasn't absolute proof, but coupled with

everything else, it was enough to convince Jessa that this woman had sold Liam. That sent her heart racing. Because each piece of this maddening puzzle pointed at only one thing—that Liam was indeed Cooper's.

"What about our other suspects—did any of them have cash withdrawals around that time matching the deposit amount that was in Sonya's account?" Cooper asked.

"I checked. Didn't find anything, though."

Probably because the buyer had made sure it couldn't be linked back to him or her, and that would have been easy enough to do for someone rich, like Donovan, or for Hector, who had a thriving law practice. For that matter, Peggy, too, could have had that amount of cash on hand so there'd be no record of it. Now the person— Peggy, Hector or Donovan—whom Sonya had entangled in this black-market-baby deal had likely murdered her or had hired someone to do the job.

Cooper stayed quiet a moment. "I'll call you back," he said to his brother. He hit the end-call button and eased back around to face her. "The person who killed her likely murdered the criminal informant, too," Cooper mumbled. "A person who has murdered twice isn't likely to stop."

Jessa wished she could disagree, but she

couldn't. "And now he or she has taken aim at Liam and us."

The *us* part she could handle. But she seriously doubted this monster wanted to kill Cooper and her and then leave her son alone. No, they wanted to sell him again or at least make sure no one could connect Liam to the illegal adoption.

"We need to do something," she whispered.

"Yeah." That was all Cooper said for several long moments. "I have a plan. You're not going to like it much, but I think this is our best shot at keeping all of us alive."

Jessa pulled in her breath, not sure she even wanted to hear this, but knowing there was no guaranteed certainty in any plan they came up with.

"Whoever's behind this wants Liam," Cooper continued. "And we can make this person think that they can have him."

"What?" Jessa couldn't say it fast enough. "We're not giving them Liam." She'd die first before she let that happen.

"No, we're not. But I want this SOB to *think* that, and here's how we'll do it." Now it was Cooper's turn to take a deep breath. "We can pretend that Liam's had some kind of complication from his surgery and that we're taking him back to the hospital—"

Jessa was shaking her head before Cooper

even finished. "I don't want Liam out there, especially at night where we wouldn't even be able to see our attackers before it was too late."

"Liam's not going anywhere," Cooper corrected. "But I am. I'll get out the word that Liam's running a fever and that I'm taking him to the E.R. Then I could make it look as if he's in the truck with me."

It didn't take Jessa long to figure out where Cooper was headed with this, and she didn't like this plan at all. "And then you'll set yourself up as bait so the kidnapper will come after you."

He darn sure didn't deny it.

"It's too dangerous," she said on a huff. "As you pointed out, this person has already murdered at least two people, and I'm sure he or she would love to add you to the list. Good grief, Cooper, this isn't a smart plan at all."

"It wouldn't be, if I didn't take precautions. Which I will. I can take one of my brothers with me, and he could stay low on the seat and out of sight."

"While you wait to be ambushed." Jessa threw her hands in the air. "What if this person just starts shooting? What chance will you have then?"

Cooper caught her shoulders. "I have a better chance of stopping this idiot than he or she does of stopping me. That's because I'm fighting for

Liam. For me this isn't about greed or covering a crime. I'll do whatever it takes to keep my son safe."

Jessa felt the same way. Whatever it took. "But this plan could backfire."

"Possibly," he admitted. "That's why I'd make sure the house is well guarded. I could move all the ranch hands near the house. They'd be armed. Plus, we'd set the security system, of course."

"And if the kidnapper is having the house watched, then he'll know that something's up."

"True," he answered so fast that it sounded as if he'd already considered that. "But I could keep the ranch hands out of sight."

Maybe. But Jessa thought of another problem with this so-called plan, and it was a huge flaw. "If I'm not with you in the truck," she said, "the kidnapper will suspect it's a trap."

Cooper stared at her a moment and then started to curse. "No way in hell will I let you go out there."

She huffed. "But you'd let yourself do this."

"Because I'm a cop. It's my job to take risks."

"This isn't a risk. It could be suicide."

"Yeah, if it's not done right. And the way to make sure it's right is to be ready. Tucker and I can be armed to the hilt, and if the kidnapper tries to force us off the road or something, we'd be right there, returning fire."

Jessa threw off his grip from her shoulders and reversed their position so that she had hold of him. She had to make him see that this wouldn't work.

Well, not without her, anyway.

"If I'm not in that truck, the kidnappers will likely just head here to the ranch. Without you around, they'll see that as their chance to find out if Liam's really here. And even if they don't manage to take him, there'll be shots fired. Do you really want Liam in the middle of a gunfight?"

"No." He backed away from her, cursed and then repeated it. "But it's only a matter of time before they try to come after him again."

"Agreed." Though it sickened her to think of her baby being in danger again. "And that's why I have to be in the truck with you. The kidnapper has to believe this is some kind of frantic rush to the hospital. That's the only thing that'll prevent him from coming here."

She could tell he wanted to argue with her, but he didn't. Instead, he paced. Cursed. And blew out another of those long breaths. Jessa knew him well enough to hear the argument going on inside his head.

An argument he was losing.

"I can't ask you to put yourself in that kind of danger," he finally said.

"You don't have to ask. Like you, I'd do anything for Liam." This definitely qualified as *anything*. "So how would we get out the word that we're on the way to the hospital?"

Still, he didn't jump to answer. Probably because he was still trying to think of another way around this. There wasn't one, and his profanity let her know he was well aware of that, too.

"How do we do it?" she pressed.

Cooper rubbed his hand over his face. "I can make a call to Doc Howland and make sure he lets everyone know we're bringing Liam into the E.R. I figure the kidnapper has someone watching the hospital."

Jessa figured the same thing. Watching the hospital, her house, the ranch and any other place that Cooper and she might go. That led Jessa to her next question.

"What if our plan causes a shoot-out at the hospital?" She cringed at the possibility of all those innocent people being caught in the cross fire.

"The idea is to find this nut job before a shoot-out can occur." But then he lifted his shoulder. "The best way to do that is to lure him and his goons away from the hospital and to the road where we can stop him."

"How? Unless you think Dr. Howland's phone line is somehow insecure."

"It's possible his line's been tapped, but we can't count on it to get the word to the kidnapper. I can use the squad radio to give Reed the false info," Cooper went on. "Then we can wait about fifteen minutes to make it look as if we're getting Liam ready to leave, and we can pretend to put him in the truck."

The squad radio was a good idea, because it wasn't secure. People tapped into them all the time. Considering how badly the kidnapper wanted them, he or she would almost certainly be listening to any communication coming in or out of the sheriff's office.

However, there was another potential problem.

"How will you get Colt to the hospital without making it look suspicious?" she asked.

"I can have him follow along behind us. It wouldn't be unusual for an uncle to go with his sick nephew to the hospital. Plus, I seriously doubt an extra lawman in tow will prevent this lunatic from coming after us." He groaned. "And that means you have to get down and stay down if anything goes wrong."

"I will, but I want to be armed, too."

That tightened his jaw muscles, because it was a reminder that this would almost certainly end in gunfire. Best-case scenario would be for them to see the kidnapper's vehicle and disable it by shooting out the tires, and then Cooper and Colt could arrest the culprit.

Worst-case scenario was for the kidnapper and

his or her hired guns to be so well hidden on the road that an attack could start before Cooper, Colt or she even knew what was happening.

Judging from his suddenly stark expression, Cooper no doubt wanted to call the whole thing off, but like her, he knew the bottom line here. There'd been two kidnapping attempts in two days. She could add her car accident to that as well, since that had likely been the first attempt.

And there would be others.

Soon.

"We're already on borrowed time," Jessa reminded him.

Cooper stayed quiet a moment, then nodded. "Come on. Let's get this started."

Chapter Sixteen

Cooper hoped he wasn't making yet another mistake tonight. Not that he was certain that sleeping with Jessa had been a mistake.

The verdict was still out on that.

But while the experience had been pretty amazing, it'd stalled him from thinking solely about how to end the danger for Liam and them. Maybe he could redeem himself with this plan.

If it worked, that was.

For that to happen, Cooper had to make sure a lot of things were in place. He'd already called Dr. Howland and Reed to get the word out that he would be bringing Liam into the E.R. He'd told the doc and Reed to be generous with spreading the news, and by now it was probably all over town that Liam had had a medical setback. That was one of the good things about living in a small town. It didn't take long for people to hear news, both good and bad.

Step two involved the ranch hands. That had

been a little trickier, since Cooper hadn't wanted to make it obvious that they were standing guard. The hands were instead keeping watch from their nearby bunkhouse but would be ready to respond if anyone tried to sneak onto the property to test if the hospital trip was some kind of ruse.

Of course, it was impossible to watch the entire ranch, so Cooper only hoped the hands would be looking in the right places at the right time if something went wrong.

Step three was for his father, Tucker, Rosalie and Rayanne to all be in position inside the house, armed and with the security system activated so they would know if someone tried to break in. Hopefully they wouldn't be needed, and while Cooper was hoping, he added a prayer that Liam would sleep through all of this. Maybe his son would even wake up in the morning without the shadow of this kidnapper looming over them.

Step four was finished, too, and it involved Colt. His brother already had weapons in his truck, but he had armed himself with more, along with putting on body armor beneath his shirt. Cooper didn't figure the kidnappers would just start shooting—if they genuinely thought Liam was in the truck—but he didn't want to take any additional risks with his kid brother.

Or with Jessa.

But she was a different matter entirely.

Yeah, he'd also had her put on body armor that she had concealed with a bulky sweater, and Cooper had given her a gun, but he wasn't even sure she could shoot well enough to defend herself. And the body armor sure wouldn't stop a shot to the head. That meant she had to stay out of the way and as safe as possible once this attack by the kidnapper started.

The final step was to get more security for the drive from the ranch to the hospital.

Easier said than done.

It'd been hard to assemble people he could trust on such short notice, but Cooper had finally called in two sheriffs from nearby towns. They wouldn't come to the ranch but rather join up with them separately on the drive to the hospital. Cooper had made it clear he didn't want them to look like lawmen and not to make it obvious that they were doing security detail. The idea was for the kidnapper to feel bold and safe enough to come after them. Jessa included.

A thought that sickened him.

After all, this kidnapper had already killed, and he or she wouldn't hesitate to do it again.

"Don't second-guess this," Jessa warned him, as if she knew exactly what he was thinking. Maybe she did. Cooper figured his expression said it all: this could be dangerous as hell.

"As long as they think Liam's in the truck, they won't shoot," she added.

Yeah, as long as the ruse worked. If it didn't, well, Cooper hoped he had enough backup security in place to stop Jessa and the others from getting hurt.

Colt's phone beeped, and he glanced down at the text that he'd just received. "It's from Reed," he relayed. "He got some deputies from Appaloosa Pass to guard the hospital, and they're getting into position now. Reed needs to know if you want them visible."

"Yes." Cooper didn't have to think about that. The last place he wanted a showdown was a hospital filled with people, and the deputies might deter that from happening.

Cooper waited until Colt had answered the text before he continued, "If we get all the way to the hospital and still haven't spotted the kidnapper, then we'll need to turn around and come back."

And come up with a different plan.

Cooper wasn't sure what that would be yet, but he didn't want these morons coming anywhere near Liam.

"You ready, then?" Colt asked.

His brother was geared up and standing by the back door. The only visible weapon he had was his sidearm, which wouldn't draw suspicion since he was a deputy, but if the kidnapper got a close look at Colt's face, then he would no doubt see the concern that was mirrored on Cooper's.

And Jessa's.

Cooper gave her one last chance. "You can stay here," he reminded her again. "And I can come up with a plausible lie to explain why you aren't coming to the hospital with us."

That earned him a huff, and she took the bundled doll from Rosalie. "No one would believe that I wouldn't be in that truck with my son. Besides, the plan's already been set into motion," Jessa insisted. "Rosalie found this doll in Rayanne's and her old room, and with the blankets around it, it'll look about the right size for Liam."

Yeah, the plan was indeed in motion, but that didn't mean Cooper had complete faith that he could keep Jessa safe. He hated that she had to be in danger, but they were both on the same page here, and that meant putting Liam and his safety first.

Cooper considered going upstairs to give Liam a kiss, but that felt too much like a goodbye. And he was determined to keep Jessa and himself alive so they could... Well, he wasn't sure what their future held, but he wanted time and the chance to figure it out without all this danger hanging over them.

Colt, Jessa and he hurried out the back and didn't waste any time getting in their respective vehicles. Jessa went through the pretense of putting the doll into a car seat. Cooper didn't miss the long look she gave the house in the side mirror as he drove away.

"Where are the sheriffs who agreed to help us?" she asked, also glancing at Colt, who was in his truck directly behind them.

Cooper hated the tremble in her voice. And her resolute expression when she took the gun he'd given her from her pocket. She was scared and determined to end this. A bad mix, and he prayed that she didn't have to take any more risks tonight.

"The first sheriff is about two miles up in a black truck. He'll pull out behind Colt and follow us into town. The second won't join us for another five miles." Still, he'd be close enough to respond if something went wrong. "He'll be in a silver-gray SUV, which should make it easy to see."

"Good." She nodded, repeated it and kept a white-knuckle grip on her gun.

Cooper took the turn from the ranch onto the farm road that led into town. Part of him was relieved that the gunmen hadn't been ready to ambush them so close to the ranch. He didn't want gunfire anywhere near Liam and the others.

But then the waiting began.

Each second crawled by while he fired glances

all around them. There were plenty of old ranch trails and farm roads where the kidnapper could lie in wait, ready to attack. He thought of Jessa's car *accident* and how fast the driver had managed to come at her. In broad daylight, no less. That was why he had to keep watch and make sure that didn't happen again. The darkness could hide a killer, and running Jessa and him off the road would make them easier targets.

"Maybe the kidnapper didn't get the word about us taking Liam to the hospital," Jessa mumbled.

Maybe. But they still had a good ten miles to go before they reached town, and they hadn't reached the most isolated part of the road yet. At the halfway point there were no farms or ranches in sight. No one to witness an attack.

Or so the kidnapper might think.

Cooper breathed a little easier when he saw the first sheriff ease onto the road behind Colt. He now had two lawmen as backup, but they still had a long way to go. It felt even longer with each mile just crawling by. Every shadow looked like a waiting killer.

His phone buzzed, the sound shooting through the truck. Through him, too. And he went on instant alert. Jessa did as well, because she sucked in her breath loud enough for him to hear. When he took it from his pocket, she darted across the seat to see the name on the screen.

Rosalie.

Hell, he hoped nothing had gone wrong with Liam. Cooper hit the answer button fast.

"I'm so sorry," Rosalie immediately said. "God, Cooper, I didn't see him before it was too late."

JESSA'S HEART SLAMMED against her chest, and she grabbed the phone away from Cooper. She prayed this was some kind of bad joke, but she knew Rosalie wouldn't joke about something like this.

"What's wrong, Rosalie? What happened?" Jessa demanded.

But Rosalie was no longer on the line.

That sent a jolt of terror and adrenaline through her. Through Cooper, too, because he hit his brakes and, with the tires squealing and smoking, made a U-turn to take them back in the direction of the ranch.

Jessa pressed the redial button, but Rosalie didn't answer. She tried again and got the same results.

Oh, God.

What was going on?

Jessa didn't like any of the possibilities that

came to mind, especially since Rosalie had said she would stay with Liam while they were gone.

I didn't see him before it was too late.

Him.

That had to be the kidnapper or one of his or her henchmen. But that didn't make sense. Cooper and she had taken plenty of security precautions to make sure no one got near Liam. So maybe Rosalie was mistaken. Or maybe Jessa had misheard her. She held on to that hope and prayed that her little boy and Rosalie were all right.

The phone buzzed again. Still no Rosalie. This time it was Colt. Both he and the sheriff had made the same U-turns and were following behind Cooper's truck, but Colt no doubt wanted to know what was going on. Jessa answered it, and because she didn't trust her voice, she held it out so that Cooper could respond.

"There's a problem at the ranch," he told Colt. "Rosalie might have been taken hostage. Maybe Liam, too."

Those words had not come easily, and they nearly sent Jessa into another panic. But she forced herself to stay calm. Well, as calm as she could manage, but they couldn't get back to the ranch fast enough.

"Call the others," Cooper added to Colt. "Find out what the hell's going on."

Cooper snatched the phone from her, ended

the call with his brother and tried to contact Rosalie again.

Still no answer.

Cooper was already going way too fast, but that caused him to speed up, and he called Tucker next. Thankfully, he answered, but Tucker's hesitation put Jessa's heart right in her throat.

"I'm not sure how it happened," Tucker finally said. "But someone got into the house...and into the room with Liam."

There was no holding back that panic now. Jessa's breath vanished, and her heart started slamming against her ribs. This was her worst nightmare come true.

"Where's Liam?" she practically shouted.

"We're not sure, but we're looking for him."

That didn't make sense. None of this did. "How did this person get in the house?"

"I don't know yet. We didn't hear anything. Didn't see anyone. There were no indications that we had an intruder. Even the security system didn't go off." Another hesitation from Tucker. "The kidnapper hit Rosalie with a stun gun, and he took Liam and your mother."

It's a good thing she wasn't standing, or her legs would have buckled. This monster had her son and her mother. A monster who'd already murdered at least two other people.

For several moments Jessa had no choice but

to give in to the terror. To allow it to paralyze her. But then the image of her son popped into her head, and she knew this fear wouldn't help. She had to think. To do something. Anything. To get Liam and her mother back.

"Did they leave the ranch?" she asked Tucker. "If they did, please tell me you're in pursuit."

But Tucker didn't get a chance to answer. Another call came through on Cooper's phone. No name or number.

Just *unknown caller* on the screen.

Jessa knew what that meant. Knew that it wouldn't be good, and she tried to brace herself. Hard to do, though, with her baby and mother missing.

"The kidnapper's calling us," Cooper told his brother, and he switched over to the new call.

Nothing.

For several snail-crawling moments. That didn't help her tamp down the panic, either.

"Cooper," the caller finally said. He or she was using some kind of voice scrambler so Jessa couldn't tell who it was. It could be any of their suspects.

Or none of them.

"You'd better not hurt my son," Cooper said through clenched teeth. Jessa shouted out the same.

"Well, that all depends on you two. Both Liam

and his grandmother will stay safe if you do as you're told."

"What do you want?" Jessa asked.

"The DNA test results. I know that Cooper has the original, and it's the only copy. I also know it's somewhere at the ranch."

It was. She'd seen it on Cooper's desk in his office.

"Bring it to the old hay barn on the back-east corner of the ranch, and I'll exchange it for Liam and Linda. You've got fifteen minutes. And if you're late or if you bring anyone else with you, the deal's off. You'll never see either of them again."

The kidnapper hadn't shouted the threat, but it certainly shouted through Jessa's mind. She had to do something to stop this now.

"Let me speak to my mother," she insisted. "I need to know they're okay."

But she was talking to the air because the kidnapper had already hung up.

"Hit Redial," Cooper told her, and he took the final turn back to the ranch.

He was going so fast that the truck skidded. For several heart-stopping moments, Jessa thought they might crash, but he managed to keep the truck on the road and sped toward the house.

Even though her hands were shaking almost

uncontrollably, Jessa managed to hit Redial. The terror skyrocketed with each unanswered ring.

Finally, she heard the voice.

"Unless you're calling to say you already have the DNA results, we have nothing to discuss," the kidnapper said.

"But we do. Let me speak to my mother. If you don't prove she's alive, you won't get that report."

It was an empty threat, but maybe the kidnapper wouldn't hear that in her voice. Even if he didn't let her talk to her mother, Cooper and she would still take the report to the barn. They'd still try to negotiate with the devil to get Liam and her mother back.

"Put my mom on the phone now," Jessa insisted, sounding a lot stronger than she felt.

It seemed to take an eternity, but she finally heard some movement. Then a voice.

"Jessa?" her mother said.

There was a split second of relief knowing her mother was still alive. Followed by the terrifying realization that the kidnapper hadn't lied. He actually had them. He had her son and her mother.

"Is Liam okay?" Jessa immediately asked.

"Yes, he fell back asleep. He doesn't know what's going on."

Jessa was beyond thankful for that and had to figure out how to get to this monster before he harmed her family. "Who kidnapped you?"

But this time there was no answer. Jessa only heard a shuffling sound and knew her mother had been moved away from the phone.

"Time's ticking away," the kidnapper said, coming back on the line.

"Who are you?" Cooper demanded.

"You'd better hope you don't have to find out. Best if I keep my identity out of this, because not knowing who I am will ensure all of you stay alive."

Jessa desperately wanted to believe that. She wanted to hang on to the hope this could all be resolved in the next few minutes and she could once again hold Liam in her arms. However, she kept going back to the reminder that they were dealing with not just a kidnapper.

But a killer.

"Get me that DNA report," the kidnapper added. "And remember the part about you coming alone—just Cooper and you. I'm using a thermal detector so I'll know if you try to bring somebody with you."

Sweet heaven. That meant Colt wouldn't be able to follow them to help. No one could.

"We'll get you the report," Jessa said, "but there's no reason to hold Liam and my mother. You're obviously already on the ranch, and you can come after us then if we don't hand over the report."

She knew she was grasping at straws, but she had to try something. Anything.

The kidnapper laughed and made a tsk-tsk sound. "I'd rather not face down a bunch of cowboy lawmen tonight. No, you and Cooper will come alone. If I see anyone else with you, your mother dies and Liam disappears forever."

Like before, the line went dead.

It took Jessa a moment just to get control of her voice so she could speak to Cooper. "What are we going to do? How do we get them back?" Because she refused to consider the alternative.

"For starters, I give this snake the DNA results," Cooper said. "Then I figure out a way to make him pay for this."

He brought the truck to a quick stop in front of the house. Tucker and his father were already on the porch, but Cooper barreled right past them. No doubt headed toward his office.

"He needs the DNA report," Jessa explained. They obviously knew what she was talking about because no one questioned her.

Rosalie stepped out of the house, and despite Tucker trying to hold her back, she hurried to Jessa. "I'm so sorry," Rosalie repeated.

Jessa nodded, and because she looked as if she needed it, she gave Rosalie's arm a pat. "Are you okay? Did the kidnapper hurt you?" she asked, eyeing the bruise on Rosalie's head.

"I'm fine." A hoarse sob left her mouth. "I'm so sorry," she repeated. "When I went to check on your mother and Liam, the kidnapper was already there in the dark room."

"Who was it?" Jessa demanded.

Rosalie shook her head and wiped away tears from her already red cheeks. Her eyes were red, too. "I don't know. The person was wearing a ski mask and used a stun gun on me. By the time I was able to get downstairs, the kidnapper already had them out of the house."

Her voice was shaking so hard it was difficult to understand her. This was no doubt bringing back horrible memories of the time her daughter was stolen.

"How did they get in?" she asked, and when Rosalie only shook her head again, Jessa looked up at Tucker.

"It looks as if someone tampered with the security system. Probably the person who broke in earlier."

Oh, God. Jessa hadn't thought that was anything more than just another failed attempt to take Liam. But the intruder had done exactly what he'd come to do.

To prepare the way for a real kidnapping.

It made her wonder what else he'd done and what he'd managed to get into place so he could get that DNA report and take Liam for good.

"So this person could have been in the house for hours," Jessa mumbled. "He could have heard everything we said about the fake trip to the hospital."

Tucker nodded, and she saw his jaw muscles at war with each other. "I'll go with you to the barn. I can hide in the truck—"

"No," Cooper said hurrying back to the truck. He had the DNA report in his hand. "He's got infrared, and he'll know if we're not alone. Plus, he'll probably have someone search the truck before we can get near him."

Tucker cursed. "You can't go out there. This is a trap and you know it."

Cooper only nodded. "Once I'm in the barn, I'll try to keep the kidnapper distracted. Use the Mylar blankets to make your way there, but put something dark over the silver so it won't be easy to see. Go on foot. The heat from another vehicle or horse could be detected."

He didn't wait for Tucker's answer. Probably because he knew his brother would do exactly as he'd said. Cooper threw the truck into gear, and the moment that Jessa was inside he hit the accelerator.

"This *is* a trap," he said, repeating Tucker's warning to them. He stayed on the dirt road that coiled around the various outbuildings on the ranch. "And this SOB will want us both dead. Probably your mother, too."

Jessa swallowed hard. She didn't want to die. Didn't want Cooper or her mother to die, either. "Liam has to come first," she insisted.

"Yeah." The emotion was there, clogging his voice. Cooper reached over and gave her hand a gentle squeeze. "No matter what happens, we get Liam out of there."

Ahead, on the horizon, Jessa saw the barn.

Chapter Seventeen

Cooper didn't have time to stop and think if this was a mistake or not. He was dead certain that it was. But he was also certain he didn't have any other choice.

Thanks to a full moon, he had a decent view of the barn. It was a good mile from the house and at the back part of the ranch. These days, the only time it got used was during hay-baling season, but since it was summer and the cattle still had fresh grass to graze on, the barn would practically be empty.

Well, except for a kidnapper, Jessa's mom and Liam.

There might be plenty of gunmen inside, too.

Cooper didn't see any sign of them. In fact, there was no sign of anyone. There didn't appear to be a light inside either, and there were no vehicles parked nearby. Of course, the property-line fence was only about fifty yards away, so it was possible the kidnapper had parked there and walked to the ranch.

The fact that no one had noticed him or her meant that the kidnapper had blended in—again. It also didn't rule out Peggy, since she could have disguised herself as one of the ranch hands.

Beside him, Jessa leaned closer to the windshield, her gaze combing the barn and surroundings. Her breath was still way too fast, and she had the same bleached-out look on her face as the day of Liam's surgery.

Yeah, she was terrified.

So was he, but along with that fear for his son, Cooper also had a massive amount of rage that he hoped he had a chance to aim at the idiot who'd set all of this in motion. Liam was in danger, again, and someone was going to pay and pay hard for that.

"See anything?" Jessa asked, and she moved her hand to the door handle. She was no doubt planning to bolt the moment he stopped.

That wasn't going to happen.

"You're to stay in the truck," he insisted. "And no, that's not negotiable, so don't argue."

She looked at him as if he'd lost his mind. "But it is *negotiable.* The kidnapper said we both have to come. If we don't, he said he'll kill my mother and Liam will disappear forever."

Cooper remembered the threat verbatim, and it would give him nightmares for years to come. However, he had to be a little sensible here and try to minimize the risks for Jessa. Even if she didn't want them minimized.

"He didn't say we both had to go in there and give him the DNA report," Cooper clarified, "only that we had to come."

At least that wasn't part of the demand that'd been spelled out. Cooper intended to use that loophole to try to buy some time for Tucker and the others to make their way to the barn. He figured they'd need at least twenty minutes, since they were traveling on foot and would have to cut through the pastures and then some wooded areas.

"We have to get Liam and my mom out," Jessa mumbled, her voice all breath and nerves, and she just kept repeating it.

Inside, he was doing the same thing.

Cooper came to a stop in front of the barn. He kept his headlights on bright and aimed them right at the closed double wood doors. Anyone peering out from the cracks might be blinded enough that they wouldn't be able to see his brother and the others. Plus, the lights gave Cooper enough illumination to see anything or anyone coming from the sides of the barns.

"Remember, you stay put," he warned Jessa.

He started to open his door, but she grabbed his arm.

She opened her mouth but didn't say anything. Not right away. "Please be careful," she finally whispered.

Cooper nodded, and because he thought they both could use it, he leaned over and brushed a kiss on her mouth. He kept it brief and tried not to notice the tears shimmering in Jessa's eyes. Those tears only ripped at his heart, and right now he had to focus on Liam and Linda.

He reached for the door again, but reaching was as far as he got. His phone rang, and he saw the now-familiar unknown caller on the screen.

The kidnapper obviously wanted to chat.

"You barely made it on time," the kidnapper snarled. "Hope you weren't talking to your kin about planning some kind of attack. FYI, that wouldn't be a smart thing to do."

Maybe not smart, but Cooper figured it was the only way he would get his son safely out of there. Yeah, it would put his brothers at risk, but if their situations were reversed, he would do the same for them.

"I've got the DNA report," Cooper said, putting the call on speaker. "And I'm bringing it to you now. Once you have it, you'll turn over the hostages to me."

The kidnapper laughed, and even though the

voice was still scrambled, that laugh managed to sound intimidating. Of course, anything at this point was unnerving since this sick dirt wad had Liam.

"Now that we've got your little fantasy scenario out of the way, here's how it's really going to work," the kidnapper said. "You and Jessa will get out of the truck and walk toward the barn. Put your weapons—*all of them*—on the ground."

"Sounds like your fantasy isn't workable with mine," Cooper snarled. "What guarantees do I have that you just won't gun us down when we get out?"

"None. But that's a chance you'll have to take. In fact, I'm betting you'll do whatever I say for a chance to get your son back."

It was the truth. Cooper knew it. So did the kidnapper. But Cooper wasn't about to say the words out loud. Jessa was already close to the breaking point, and there was no need to spell out that this could go wrong. Fast.

"Now get out of the truck," the kidnapper continued. "And if you broke the rules and brought someone with you, I'll know."

Cooper heard the whirring sound, and he spotted the camera on the eaves of the barn. It certainly wasn't something his family had installed, so the kidnapper had likely brought it with him. The camera turned slowly, no doubt so the kidnapper could see the truck bed and what was inside.

"Good. You listened to that come-alone part," the kidnapper said several moments later.

"We've done everything you asked," Cooper reminded him. "Now let them go."

"All in due time. Maybe I'll give you a gold star for following the rules. Now, don't forget the really big rule about putting the guns on the ground," the kidnapper added.

Cooper had every intention of doing that. Well, one of his weapons, anyway. He had another in the back waist of his jeans, and he hoped he'd be able to get to it in time if he needed it.

And he figured he would need it.

Jessa was another matter. Even though there were some other weapons in the glove compartment, Jessa only had one gun. One that he wasn't even sure she could use, and in her case, being armed might turn out to be a detriment. If the kidnapper just planned to shoot them on sight, then Jessa wouldn't get a chance to draw, anyway. And if she tried to keep the gun on her and the kidnapper saw it, then Jessa could be shot just for breaking a *rule*. They could be damned if they did or damned if they didn't.

Cooper held his hand over the phone so the kidnapper wouldn't be able to hear what he was about to say to her. "When we get out, toss your gun toward the barn and then stay behind the truck door."

It wasn't ideal protection, but along with the body armor, it might be enough. Might.

"You'll stay behind the truck door, too," Jessa insisted.

Maybe. But Cooper doubted this SOB would allow that. It was going to be hard enough just to get that concession for Jessa.

He took his hand from the phone. "We're getting out of the truck now," Cooper informed the kidnapper.

With the DNA report tucked under Cooper's arm, he and Jessa opened their doors together and both stepped out. Almost at the same time, they tossed their guns in front of the barn.

And they waited.

"Move out so I can see you," the kidnapper said.

Cooper huffed. "Give me proof that my son and Mrs. Wells are all right. And if they aren't, don't expect to get out of this alive. Because I will kill you."

Another laugh. It made Cooper wish he could tear through the barn wall and beat this idiot senseless. He still might get a chance to do that before this was over.

"Proof of life," the kidnapper continued after

the laughter had died down. "Still think you're the one calling the shots here?"

Cooper's phone dinged, and he looked down at the screen. It was a text from Tucker.

Found a gunman near the house. He's been neutralized. Am on the way.

Cooper didn't want to risk texting back because he didn't want to take his attention off the kidnapper, but it was good news. One down and heaven knew how many to go.

"You don't get the report, or us, if we don't have proof that Liam's alive," Cooper argued with the kidnapper. "Or maybe you should consult your henchmen to make sure you have plenty of help keeping me under control."

Silence.

Cooper wasn't sure the kidnapper would actually hear the veiled threat, but the silence could mean the person was trying to get in touch with the gunman. The one Tucker had already neutralized.

"What's the matter?" Cooper asked. "Is your hired gun not answering?"

More silence. He didn't want the kidnapper to get desperate and start shooting, but he also wanted the idiot to understand he was on his own here.

Well, maybe.

Maybe there was only one other gunman, but if there were more, Cooper hoped his brothers would find them. He wanted to focus just on the jerk in the barn and not worry about being ambushed.

"I want some proof of life," Cooper reminded him.

"Okay," the scrambled voice finally said. Maybe it was his imagination, but the kidnapper didn't seem nearly as confident as when they'd first arrived. "You'll get that proof. And since I don't want to stand around here and nitpick, you and Jessa step away from the truck at the same moment that the barn door opens. My advice? Don't shoot, because it won't be me standing there."

Cooper heard some movement, and it didn't take long before he heard the creaking sound of the hinges. The barn door eased open.

"Don't go out there," Cooper whispered to Jessa.

Maybe, just maybe, he could keep her hidden away enough to find out what they were up against. He still didn't know how much backup the kidnapper had in there with him.

Thankfully, Jessa did as he told her. She stayed hidden behind the door, but Cooper moved as fast as he could. He still had his phone in his left hand, but he wanted to have his shooting hand clear in case he had to fire.

"Jessa?" someone called out.

It was Linda, and a moment later the woman appeared in the doorway. She had Liam bundled in a blanket in her arms.

"Mom," Jessa said, but thankfully she stayed put.

The truck headlights blazed on Linda like a spotlight, and while she didn't appear to be injured, she was pasty white and shaking. She had clearly been through an ordeal since she'd been in the barn with a killer for the past half hour.

Cooper couldn't see Liam; the blanket completely covered him. Nor could he see the kidnapper. The person remained in the shadows near the door, but Cooper could see enough of the outline that he knew where to aim if he got the chance to take out this moron.

"Tell Linda to move now," the kidnapper said to Cooper from over the phone, and Cooper relayed that to her.

Linda gave a shaky nod, and she walked out of the barn. Not far, though. Just a few steps away from the front of the barn and directly in Cooper's path. Whoever this jerk was, he or she knew what to do by keeping Linda in the line of fire. No way would Cooper risk taking a shot when Linda or his son could be hurt.

"Now, Jessa, it's your turn," the kidnapper said, his voice taunting through the phone. "You want to see your baby boy, don't you? Well, have a look and you'll see that he's as right as rain."

Still trembling, Linda shook her head just a little. Just enough for Cooper's stomach to twist into a knot.

And that was when he saw the glint of metal from the kidnapper's gun. Aimed not at him.

But right at Jessa.

"DON'T GO OUT THERE," Cooper warned her again.

Even though he'd only whispered it, Jessa heard Cooper's warning loud and clear, but the last thing she wanted to do was stay put.

She had to get to her son.

"If you go out there, he'll kill you," Cooper told her when she started away from the truck.

That wouldn't have stopped her, but the sound of the kidnapper's voice did.

"Your son and mother aren't in any real danger, *yet,*" the kidnapper said through the phone scrambler.

"Yet," she repeated.

The threat was clear—the danger would be worse if she didn't cooperate. It chilled her. Angered her. And sent a dozen other emotions through her.

Part of her wished she could hurt this person

the way he was hurting her while another part of her only wanted to shout for her mother to start running so that Liam and she could maybe get out of there.

"Well?" the kidnapper prompted. "I've kept my part of the bargain, and you two need to keep yours by coming out from behind that truck."

Jessa glanced at Cooper, and she knew from his expression that they were on the same wavelength here. The kidnapper would almost certainly gun them down when they stepped out.

And Liam and her mother would be caught in the middle.

She had no idea what they could do to defuse this, but Jessa gasped when Cooper stepped out.

Right into the line of fire.

Jessa nearly went after him, but Cooper shot her a stay-put glare, and he made his way toward the barn doors.

"Where should I put this DNA report?" Cooper asked.

She saw the gun in the back waist of his jeans, and Cooper kept his right hand by his side so he could hopefully get to it in time.

"Bring it to me," the kidnapper insisted. "Jessa and you together."

"Why do you need Jessa for this? Don't you want to see the report first?" Cooper asked. "To make sure it's the real deal."

"It is. You wouldn't be stupid enough to bring me a fake."

Cooper lifted his shoulder. "I might if I didn't trust you. Or if I thought you didn't have any backup gunmen with you."

What the heck was Cooper doing? He shouldn't be antagonizing this person. Or did he have some other plan up his sleeve that she didn't know about?

Cooper cautiously walked to the doors and positioned himself between her mother and the kidnapper. Cooper turned his head a little and whispered something to her mother. Something that Jessa didn't catch.

"Here," Cooper said, holding out the report.

"Come closer," the kidnapper snapped.

And Cooper did. Jessa held her breath, praying and waiting. Her mother appeared to be praying, too, and she had her attention fixed not on Jessa, but on something over Jessa's shoulder.

"Now," she heard Cooper say.

Her mother ducked down, and with Liam still cradled in her arms, she scrambled to the side of the barn. Cooper quickly followed them. Out of the line of fire.

Maybe.

But Jessa was terrified the kidnapper would just start shooting and that the bullets would go through the wooden-plank siding on the barn.

The kidnapper didn't shoot, but he let out a string of profanity. Definitely male, but his voice was still partly muffled. He no longer sounded like the cocky person who'd first spoken to him. He was quickly coming unhinged, and that could be bad news for them. Of course, not much about this was good news, except that maybe her mother and Liam were now in a better position to get away.

"What's the matter?" Cooper called out. "Where's your backup?"

There was only one reason that Cooper would keep bringing that up—someone had managed to find the kidnapper's henchman and had stopped him. That explained the message Cooper had gotten right before her mother had stepped out of the barn.

"You think I don't have someone else out there who can help me handle this?" the kidnapper said. But he didn't sound confident about that, either.

The kidnapper was no longer using the scrambler, but she thought maybe he had a cloth or something over his mouth. No doubt still trying to protect his identity.

While keeping her head low, Jessa looked around, hoping to see if she could spot any of henchmen or Cooper's family, but the only thing she saw was the darkness.

"Time's up," the kidnapper barked. "If Jessa and you don't come out now, this is over."

"You haven't even looked at the report yet," Cooper said immediately. "Why have me bring it all the way out here if you're not even going to look at it?"

"Oh, I think you know why you're here. I could have broken into the house and stolen that report at any time."

That chilled her to the bone. Because she knew it was true. "You were watching the place," she said, and even though she was scared, there was plenty of anger in her voice.

"Watching through cameras. You people really should have given the house a good once-over after the break-in. My assistant managed to put a few bugs and cameras in place."

The chill turned to a sickening feeling. This monster had spied on them.

"I think your mom might be surprised to know that you're sleeping with the sheriff," the kidnapper went on. "Do you think that'll maybe convince him to let you keep Liam? I think not," he said before she could speak.

In fact, she didn't get a chance to do anything.

"Time's up," the kidnapper repeated.

And the person stumbled out of the barn.

Chapter Eighteen

Cooper saw Peggy the moment she came out, and he also saw the gun she had gripped in her hand. He shoved his phone in his pocket and nearly fired, but something caused him to hesitate.

It was the dazed look on Peggy's face.

Something was wrong.

However, Cooper didn't get a chance to figure out exactly what before the shot zinged through the air.

"Get down!" Cooper shouted to Jessa, and he prayed she would do just that.

He pushed Linda farther back and leaned out, ready to return fire.

But there wasn't another shot.

Peggy stood there, still dazed, her gun pointed at the ground. She certainly hadn't been the one to fire. Cooper could see that even though she was indeed holding a gun, her hands were tied with clear plastic cuffs. Maybe the kidnapper had figured Cooper would shoot her first and ask questions later.

If he had, Peggy would have been dead, and he might have killed an innocent woman.

Jessa was still crouching behind the truck door, but she glanced at Cooper, her expression asking if he knew what was going on. He only shook his head and motioned for her to get down. As long as they stayed out of range, the kidnapper wouldn't be able to get to them. Not all at once, anyway. And if he started shooting at Jessa, Cooper was in a position to return fire.

At least he would be if Peggy got out of his way.

"I didn't do anything wrong," Peggy said, her words slurred. It sounded as if she'd been drugged. "Please help me—"

Another shot blasted through the air. Again, not from Peggy's gun. Cooper could see that her trigger finger hadn't moved.

But Peggy certainly did.

The woman made a raspy sound that came deep from within her throat, and the gun slipped from her hand and to the ground. A second later, Peggy crumpled in a heap next to it.

It was only then that Cooper saw the dark stain spreading across her shirt. *Blood.* She'd been shot in the back. If she wasn't already dead, she soon would be. He had to get an ambulance out here, but even that was too risky.

"Told you time was up," the kidnapper taunted. He was still inside the barn.

"You didn't have to kill her!" Jessa shouted.

"Yeah, actually, I did." His voice was shaky now. Maybe because killing a woman had gotten to him or maybe he was coming to realize that his plan was falling apart. "She could have maybe linked me back to Liam."

Maybe.

And if he would kill on a *maybe,* then he'd damn sure kill Jessa and him if he got the chance. Not just Jessa and him, either, but anyone who might connect him to the crimes, including Linda and even Liam, since Liam's own DNA proved that he'd been stolen and put up for adoption.

"I want you to run," Cooper whispered to Linda. "Stay on this side of the barn, away from that camera. Keep Liam close to you and stay low."

Linda gave a shaky nod, and the moment she took off running, Cooper leaned out from the corner of the barn and hoped the sound of his movements would cover any noise that Linda was making during her escape.

"So are you Hector or Donovan?" Cooper asked. He figured any distraction would help right now. Help Linda get to cover and give his brothers time to arrive.

"Come in here and you can see for yourself," the kidnapper growled.

Cooper watched as Linda ducked behind a tree. It wasn't ideal cover, but it got her away from the barn, and the tree might be able to stop any bullets fired in that direction.

His phone dinged again, and Cooper ducked back around the side of the barn so the kidnapper wouldn't notice what he was doing. He saw the text that he'd been waiting for.

Second gunman caught, Tucker wrote. I can see your truck lights from where I'm standing, and there are no other gunmen around.

Get Linda and Liam out of here, Cooper texted back. He would have loved to include Jessa in that rescue, but it was too risky.

Liam had to be rescued first.

Plus, Jessa was still too close to the shooter. If Tucker tried to get to her, Jessa and he would just be gunned down like Peggy.

"I want you to give me that DNA report now!" the kidnapper yelled.

Yeah, the guy was definitely losing it, probably because he knew both of his hired guns were out of commission. Were there more? Maybe. But if so, Cooper hoped this idiot called his backup to the barn so it would give Tucker a safer path to escape with Linda and Liam.

Without warning, a shot rang out and blasted into his truck.

Cooper's heart went to the ground, and he quickly looked to make sure Jessa hadn't been hit. He saw her scramble back into the truck and across the seat. Good. He hoped she'd stay there.

But she didn't.

When the kidnapper fired again, Jessa stuck her hand out from the open door. Cooper saw the gun she held. One that she'd no doubt taken from the glove compartment.

Jessa pulled the trigger. The bullet slammed into the barn door, and she didn't stop there. She fired another shot. Then another.

"Big mistake!" the kidnapper yelled, and he called her a name mixed with some raw profanity. He made a sound of outrage, the kind of sound a crazy man would make, and the shots started coming.

Nonstop.

The bullets began to pelt the truck, ripping through the glass, one of the headlights and the metal, and Cooper knew it was only a matter of time before one of the shots hit Jessa.

Hell. That couldn't happen. It couldn't end like this.

She didn't give up and sure as heck didn't get

down on the seat. Jessa returned fire until she ran out of ammunition, and judging from what Cooper could see of her, she then began to rifle through the glove compartment for more.

"Stay down!" Cooper yelled to her, and he started running. Toward the back of the barn.

His best bet was to sneak up on this guy and take him out. Maybe he'd be alone, but if not, Cooper would have to deal with that, too.

With only one headlight left on his truck, it was hard to see, but Cooper made it to the back of the barn. The doors were shut, of course. Fate wasn't going to make this easy. But he peeked through the cracks in the wood.

Just as the shots stopped.

Cooper heard the movement then.

Footsteps.

Not near the back of the barn. But the front. He saw the doors there fly open. And Cooper knew he'd just made a huge mistake coming back here.

Cooper started running toward his truck. Toward Jessa. But the fear slammed right into him when he spotted her. Not inside the bullet-riddled truck where he'd last spotted her. But outside, several yards away from it.

The kidnapper was behind her and had her at gunpoint.

"I'M SORRY," JESSA SAID, the fear obvious in her voice and in every part of her body. Not fear for herself, but for Cooper, her mother and her son. She hadn't wanted it to come down to this, because the kidnapper could use her to draw out Cooper.

Cooper gave her a glance and took cover beside the barn. He leaned out, his gaze connecting with hers. It was hard to see his expression, but she knew he was feeling the same thing that she was.

"Please tell me that Liam is safe," she managed to say.

"He's safe," Cooper assured her, without taking his attention or aim off the man behind her.

She still hadn't seen her captor's face because he'd been wearing a ski mask when he'd first come at her and dragged her from the truck. However, the mask had come off in the struggle when Jessa had managed to get out of the truck and run.

She hadn't gotten far before he'd caught up with her.

"Liam's safe *for now,*" the man snarled. He had something over his mouth, a bandanna, and it was muffling his voice. "It won't stay that way if I have anything to do with it."

She wasn't immune to that threat. Every word

hit her like a fist, and she hated that this monster had any say in what would happen to her son.

"You don't need to disguise your voice any longer," Cooper challenged him. "And you don't need to hide behind Jessa. Let her go, and we'll deal with this—just you and me."

The man didn't say anything else, but he was moving. Not in the direction of the barn but rather back to the truck. God, was he planning on trying to use it to escape with her? A hostage could get him off the ranch. Of course, he'd try to kill Cooper and his brothers first.

"Donovan," Cooper spat out like profanity. He was staring right at the man and could no doubt see Donovan's face.

Jessa's stomach clenched even more. If the kidnapper had been Hector, she thought she could have reasoned with him. Maybe by offering him money. But Donovan hated Cooper, and that made this attack personal. Donovan wouldn't stop because of anything she might say.

"Let her go," Cooper repeated.

"Not likely." Donovan shoved the bandanna from his mouth. "She's my ticket out of here. My ticket to freedom."

Jessa tried to elbow him in the stomach, but he curved his arm around her neck and yanked her back. He put so much pressure on her windpipe that she thought she might lose consciousness.

Not good. Because she had to be able to fight if she got the chance.

"Why the hell did you take my son?" Cooper asked. The pain was in his voice. His face. Every part of his body. He was no doubt reliving the horrible memories of losing his wife and believing his son had been lost, too.

"This isn't a good time for conversation." Donovan eased up the pressure on her neck. Probably because he didn't want to have to carry an unconscious woman. Besides, she was only of use to him if her body shielded his.

From the corner of her eye, she saw Donovan glance all around them. Yes, she was his human shield, but that wouldn't prevent one of Cooper's brothers from attacking him from behind. Jessa prayed that would happen before Donovan got a chance to kill Cooper.

And Donovan would do that.

She needed to do something to give Cooper and herself a fighting chance, so she dug in her heels when Donovan continued to drag her back toward the truck.

"I want to know," Cooper tossed out there, "what was going through your head two years ago when you found out Liam was alive."

"*You* were going through my head!" Donovan practically shouted. "You and Molly, and the way you treated me. You deserved to lose them both. The flood took Molly, and I got your son."

Cooper's expression didn't change, but she figured the words had to hit him like fists, too. "How did Sonya Eakins know to bring Liam to you?"

"Why does it matter?"

"It matters." Cooper paused and took a deep breath. "It hurts to hear it, but I want to know."

"It hurts?" Donovan snarled, his tone taunting again. "Well, then, I wish I had a million details to give you. And to crush you. Sonya worked for me, briefly and off the books. She knew how much I hated you, so after she found the kid, she came to me."

"How did she know Liam was mine?"

"She saw Molly's car, recognized it." Jessa couldn't be sure, but she thought Donovan might be smiling. It nearly made her gag. "Go ahead and ask if Sonya could have saved Molly."

"Could she have saved her?" Cooper's voice sounded as strangled as Jessa felt.

Donovan laughed, obviously enjoying this little torture session. "No. She got there too late for that. She only found the kid. She thought I'd want to use the baby to get you to cough up lots and lots of money. But I figured that'd be too easy, and I didn't want you to have any part of Molly."

Yes, definitely like fists. It crushed her, too,

because she'd been part of this monster's plan and hadn't even known it. Jessa didn't regret adopting Liam, but she hated the pain this had caused Cooper.

"Now come on out," Donovan demanded, "and take your punishment like a man."

"Cooper didn't do anything to be punished," Jessa reminded him. It only caused Donovan to jam the gun harder against her head.

For a second, anyway.

Then he turned the gun. Took aim at Cooper.

And fired.

The sound blasted through her and would have brought her to her knees if Donovan hadn't kept a firm grip on her. It took her a few moments to realize the bullet had torn through a chunk of the barn, but it hadn't hit Cooper. Thank God he was all right.

For now.

Donovan kept looking around them, kept maneuvering her to the truck. She figured he couldn't just kill her because he'd lose his protection, so Jessa kept struggling despite the choke hold he put on her.

"You planted evidence to make Peggy and Hector look guilty," Cooper said, glancing around the corner again.

Donovan fired another shot.

Mercy, this had to stop, but the more she

fought, the more Donovan fought, too. If he got her into that truck and off the ranch, he would no doubt use her to bargain with Cooper. Maybe to keep Cooper silent or to get him to obstruct justice or something.

Either way, Donovan would kill her when he was finished with her.

"Taking me won't get you Liam," Jessa reminded him. "Cooper won't trade him for me. Nor would I want him to."

"I don't need Cooper to choose between his son and you," Donovan insisted. "Though since he's your lover, that would be a nice way to give the knife another twist."

The man was sick, along with being a sadistic killer. Cooper probably hadn't known just how much Donovan hated him, but he certainly knew it now.

"What about the DNA report?" Cooper shouted. When he glanced around the corner again, Donovan fired another shot at him. Each bullet ate away more of the barn and more of Cooper's cover. "You wanted it badly enough to demand that I bring it to you."

"That was then and this is now. I don't care if you have proof that Liam's yours. Don't care what happens to him or you. Time for me to regroup, but trust me, this isn't over. I'll be back to finish this."

She'd doubted some of the other things that Donovan had said, but Jessa didn't doubt that last part. If he managed to escape, he would indeed kill her and then come back. For Cooper and Liam. For anyone who'd gotten in his way. And next time, Cooper might not be able to keep Liam out of this monster's path.

Donovan gave her a fierce jerk and climbed onto the truck seat, dragging Jessa right along with him. Despite all the glass littering the seat, he got behind the wheel and kept her positioned between Cooper and himself.

He fired another shot at Cooper, enough to get him to duck back behind cover. Then Donovan started the engine.

Oh, God. He was getting away.

Jessa looked around for anything she might be able to use as a weapon. Her fingers closed around a large piece of glass from the windshield, and she brought it up to jab it in his eye.

She didn't get far.

As if he'd known all along what she planned, Donovan knocked the glass away, and in the same motion he drove his elbow into her chin. He hit her so hard that Jessa not only lost her breath, she saw stars. She had to fight hard to stop herself from losing consciousness.

Donovan loosened the grip he had on her

slightly, and he didn't waste even a second before he slammed his foot on the accelerator.

And he drove the truck right at Cooper.

Chapter Nineteen

Cooper didn't have time to think. He could only react. He dived to his right, barely in time. The truck's fender bumped into him, but he managed to stay on his feet.

He got just a glimpse of Jessa then. At the stark terror on her face. Donovan still had his left arm hooked around her neck, and even though he was holding his gun in his right, he somehow managed to get off another shot.

Cooper had lost count of how many shots Donovan had fired, but he prayed the man ran out of ammunition soon. While he was praying, he added that Tucker had managed to rescue Liam and Linda. There'd been no other texts from his brother, and he hoped nothing had gone wrong.

With Donovan, anything was possible.

Cooper had always known the man hated him, but he'd had no idea just how much until tonight. Donovan wanted to make him suffer in the worst way possible and then kill him. Jessa, too. And it didn't seem to matter that others would know of his guilt. Donovan was just hell-bent on getting even for what he considered an old, unforgivable wrong—Molly no longer loving him.

"Watch out!" Jessa shouted to Cooper when Donovan turned the steering wheel, aiming the truck right at Cooper again.

Cooper didn't want to run toward the tree where he'd last seen Linda and Liam. They could still be there or nearby, and it was too big a risk to take. There was no other nearby cover, so Cooper went behind the barn instead.

Donovan followed right along behind him. So close that Cooper could feel the heat from the engine on his back and legs. He couldn't risk shooting at the SOB because he could accidentally hit Jessa. She was already in too much danger without him adding more. However, Cooper did aim for one of the tires. He missed.

Cooper made it around the barn, hoping it would take Donovan several seconds at least to maneuver the vehicle. It didn't. Despite being hindered by a struggling Jessa and a weapon clutched in his hand, Donovan just kept coming.

And he fired another shot.

This was one didn't hit the barn, and it put Cooper's heart right in his throat. Liam was out there somewhere, and that bullet could have come close to him.

Or worse.

Cooper got back to the front of the barn, and he ducked around Peggy's lifeless body and inside the still-open doors. Maybe when Donovan reached him, Cooper could somehow get Jessa out.

However, Donovan didn't slow down enough. Nor did he turn away from the barn.

He swerved around Peggy, and the truck bashed through the doors and came right at Cooper. He had no choice but to run again and try to get back outside. If he stayed inside, Donovan could hit one of the thick posts while trying to get him, and since Jessa wasn't wearing a seat belt, she could be thrown through what was left of the windshield.

Jessa screamed, and Cooper glanced over his shoulder to see her sink her teeth into Donovan's arm. The man cursed and let go of the steering wheel so he could bash the gun against her head.

Cooper could have sworn that he saw red.

Cooper darted to the side, hoping he could still try to pull Jessa from the truck. But Donovan regained control. Not just of the steering wheel but also his weapon.

He fired at Cooper.

And this time Cooper wasn't so lucky at dodging bullets. The pain sliced through his arm.

Hell. He'd been hit.

He couldn't take the time to figure out how badly he was injured, because the truck was coming right for him again. Worse, Jessa was dazed or something. Her eyes were half-closed, and she looked ready to faint. Donovan had obviously hurt her when he'd hit her.

And that made him a dead man.

Cooper couldn't stop the shout that roared from his throat, and he turned, not to get away from the truck. But rather to face it head-on. He took aim, praying he had a clear shot so he could stop Donovan for good.

Donovan came right at him as if he was playing a game of chicken. Cooper cursed because he still didn't have a clean shot.

"Be seeing you," Donovan said, smiling.

He gave the steering wheel a sharp turn to the right and plowed through the back door. The splintered wood burst out like daggers, some of them slicing across Cooper's face, but they didn't stop him. He barreled out the gaping hole and hurried outside.

Donovan was getting away.

Cooper hadn't thought that knot in his stomach could get any tighter, but he'd obviously been wrong. Donovan was taking Jessa God knew where, and there was no telling what the man would do to her to get back at Cooper.

Again, he couldn't shoot because he had no

idea where Liam and the others were. But Cooper started running. He had to get to the truck before Donovan managed to get off the ranch. He took out his phone, and without slowing down, he hit the button to call Tucker.

"Don't let Donovan get away," Cooper insisted, and he shoved his phone back in his pocket in case he had to fire.

His heart was already racing, but it started to pound against his chest. It only got worse when he heard Jessa scream again. Cooper could only see shadowy movements in the cab of the truck, but it looked as if Jessa was in another fight with Donovan.

And then Cooper heard the shot.

This bullet hadn't come at him; he was pretty sure it'd stayed in the cab of the truck.

Hell.

Had Donovan shot Jessa?

That only made Cooper run faster, even though he knew he'd have a hard time catching up with the now-speeding truck. That didn't stop him. No way. Somehow he had to get to Jessa and make sure she was all right.

Ahead of him, he saw the bloodred flash of the brake lights, and it took Cooper a moment to figure out why Donovan had done that. But there were several horses in the pasture, and Donovan had nearly run right into them. If he had, it would have not only injured or killed the horses, it would have disabled the truck. That was probably the only reason he hadn't crashed into them.

That delay gave Cooper some much-needed seconds so he could close the distance between him and the truck. Even over the engine, he heard Donovan curse. Saw more of the struggle going on in the cab.

Thank God.

It meant Jessa was alive, but she wouldn't stay that way for long.

Cooper was still running when he saw the truck door fly open, and he caught just a glimpse of Jessa trying to get out before Donovan hit her with the gun again. He dragged her back inside with him, slammed the door.

"Jessa!" Cooper yelled, just so she'd know that he was close. He wanted her to keep fighting. Wanted her to stay alive so he could get to her.

Donovan must have realized it, too, because he floored the accelerator. Maybe it was because of the struggle going on inside the truck.

Or maybe Donovan suddenly had a death wish.

Either way, Cooper could only watch as the truck slammed right into a tree.

JESSA WAS SO caught up in her fight to get away from Donovan that she didn't see the tree in time to brace herself for the impact.

Not that she could have done much.

She wasn't wearing a seat belt. However, she was squeezed against the driver's-side door and Donovan, and he was the one who went through the windshield first. Jessa wasn't far behind. She smashed into him.

The pain slammed through her, so hard and fast that it blurred her vision and knocked the breath out of her. She did a quick assessment and didn't think she was hurt too badly. But Cooper could be a different story. She'd seen the shot that Donovan had fired at him in the barn.

And she'd seen the blood.

He was hurt. Maybe it was a serious injury, and she had to get to him to see if he needed help.

Jessa forced herself to get moving. Not easy to do. Both Donovan and she were on what was left of the hood of the truck, and they were wedged against the tree. Worse, Donovan had somehow managed to hang on to his gun. She reached for it, but that was as far as she got.

Donovan's eyes flew open, snaring her in his gaze.

God, no.

He should be dead or at least unconscious, but here he was ready to attack her all over again. And try one more time to kill Cooper. He latched on to her wrist, digging his fingernails into her skin.

And he fired.

The shot blasted past her, but she knew it could have hit someone. Maybe Cooper. Heaven forbid, maybe Liam. It crushed her heart to think of her baby being hurt, and all because of this monster and his hatred.

"Jessa?" she heard Cooper call out, and she spotted him running toward her. He was alive, thank God, but even in the milky moonlight, she could see the blood on his shirt.

"Donovan's still armed," she warned Cooper. He was close, but not close enough to stop Donovan from getting off another shot. She had to be the one to stop him, or this time he might succeed in killing Cooper or her.

Jessa rammed her elbow against the man's jaw, and while it wasn't enough to loosen the gun, it did cause him to let go of her. She didn't have much wiggle room, but she used her hands and feet to get some leverage, pushing herself away from the truck, the tree and him.

She made it the rest of the way through the broken windshield and was finally able to roll off the hood.

She didn't land on her feet. She was too woozy for that and instead fell to her knees, but Jessa got up as quickly as she could.

However, it wasn't fast enough.

Donovan slid off right behind her.

Just like before, he put the gun to her head, and

he ducked down behind her. Unlike before, Cooper didn't have the cover of the barn to protect him. He was out in the open, running toward her.

"Get down!" Jessa shouted.

She braced herself for Donovan to fire again. But he didn't. Maybe because he was running low on ammunition. He'd already fired a lot of shots.

"Let her go," Cooper ordered. He stopped about ten yards away from them and took aim. Not that he could shoot. She was in the way again, and Donovan did his best to keep hidden behind her.

"You're not going to win this time," Donovan spat out, the venom heavy in his voice.

Cooper shook his head. "Your beef's with me, not Jessa. Let her go."

"Right, so you can just gun me down," Donovan snarled back. "By my calculations, I have just one bullet left. I've got extra ammo in my pocket, but by the time I got to it, it'd be too late."

"Yeah, it would," Cooper assured him, and he inched closer. He bracketed his right wrist with his left hand. "And that's why you need to put down your gun and surrender. It's over, Donovan."

That wasn't the right thing to say. She felt the muscles in Donovan's body turn to iron again, and his breath rushed out like fire.

"It's never over!" Donovan shouted. "I could live as long as I knew you were grieving every single day. But you're not grieving now, are you? You're sleeping with Jessa, knowing it'll help you breeze through getting custody of your son."

Cooper took another step, held his aim. "Not that it's any of your business, but that's not why I slept with her."

Donovan laughed. "Please," he said, stretching that out a few syllables. "You haven't looked at another woman since Molly. You've been moping around town, all dark and tortured. Just the way I wanted you to feel."

Cooper didn't argue with that. "You made sure I felt that way by kidnapping my son and keeping him from me."

"Yes, I did." Donovan sounded pleased, but Jessa heard another sound. He was shifting the gun, no doubt so he could aim it at Cooper. He'd said he only had one bullet, but one was enough.

"Ironic, though, that you'd figure out a way to get your son back," Donovan snarled, "and replace Molly at the same time."

Despite the pain from the wreck and Donovan's blows with the gun, that riled her to the core. "I'll never replace Molly," she fired back.

In fact, she couldn't be sure that Cooper hadn't slept with her just because of Liam. He wouldn't have done it intentionally.

No, he was too honorable for that.

But Cooper could have been drawn to her simply because he was so thankful to have found his little boy. It would be easier on her heart if it'd been the same for her, if her feelings for Cooper had been because of Liam.

But they weren't.

Jessa could see that now. She knew that she cared deeply for Cooper, despite the fact that if they survived this, he might take Liam from her.

"Time's up," Donovan repeated. "No more happy times for you." And he raised the gun to fire at Cooper.

Just as Jessa dropped to the ground.

The men fired their guns at the same time, and the combined blasts created a thundering boom that seemed to echo through the darkness. Jessa was terrified to look in case Donovan had hit his intended target. Terrified also that Cooper hadn't hit his.

She lifted her head, but she didn't even get a glimpse of Cooper before Donovan slumped against her, knocking her face-first to the ground.

"Jessa?" Cooper called out.

She was still fighting to get Donovan off her when Cooper made it to her and pulled away the dead weight so she could scramble back and stand. Jessa saw him then. Donovan's lifeless eyes fixed in a blank stare.

Unlike Cooper's.

There was plenty of life and concern in his eyes, and he slipped his arm around her and pulled her to him. He brushed what had to be a kiss of relief on her forehead before his gaze fired all around.

Mercy. He was looking for Liam and her mother. They definitely weren't by the tree any longer, but she couldn't see them anywhere in the pasture.

"Where's Liam?" she managed to ask.

But Cooper just shook his head. "Come on. We have to find him."

Chapter Twenty

Cooper ignored the throbbing in his arm and scooped Jessa up so he could get her away from Donovan and find Liam. Jessa had already seen too much blood tonight, and there was no need for her to see more.

"Tucker?" he called out.

No answer, so he managed to take out his phone and handed it to Jessa. "Call my brother."

They'd been through hell and back, but there was no worse hell than not knowing if their son was all right.

He mentally repeated that: *their son.*

And while it packed an emotional wallop, Cooper decided to table it for now. The only thing that mattered was getting to Liam and then making sure that everyone was okay.

That included Jessa.

She was bleeding on her hands and face. Hopefully just minor nicks and cuts, but he wouldn't know for sure until the doctor had checked her out.

"He's not answering," Jessa said. She was shaking all over, maybe even going into shock.

Cooper could hear the rings on the other end of the line, and he held his breath until he finally heard something he wanted to hear. Tucker's voice.

But not on the phone.

"Over here," Tucker called out to them. Cooper spotted his brother holding a flashlight, halfway between them and the house.

"Where's Liam?" Cooper and Jessa asked at the same time.

"He's here with me," Linda answered. "We're both okay."

The relief nearly brought him to his knees, but Cooper kept running and Jessa slipped out of his arms so they could go even faster together.

As they got closer, Cooper could see Tucker and Colt. And the man kneeling on the ground. One of Donovan's hired guns, no doubt. He'd been cuffed, and Colt was holding him at gunpoint.

Linda stepped from Colt's truck with Liam in her arms. His little boy was still sacked out, thank God. He hadn't seen any of this horrible mess.

"We got both gunmen," Colt volunteered. "One didn't make it." He tipped his head toward the barn nearest the house. "The ME's on the way to get the body."

"Bodies," Cooper corrected. "Donovan's dead, too."

Other than some sounds of relief, no one had much of a reaction to that. Good. Cooper didn't want to give Donovan anything, especially not a lifetime of anger over what he'd done. Donovan had already claimed enough by keeping Liam from him all this time, and he'd given them enough nightmares. Especially Jessa.

"Peggy's dead, as well," Cooper explained. "I'm pretty sure Donovan kidnapped her and brought her here. Her hands are cuffed, and she appeared to have been drugged."

And with Peggy, that meant Donovan had murdered at least three people. All to get back at him and cover his tracks.

"You're hurt," Tucker said, glancing Cooper's arm.

It was just a flesh wound. He'd deal with that later, too, but for now he and Jessa hurried to Liam. They both reached for him at the same time, but Jessa froze and drew back her hands.

Oh, man.

He didn't want her to feel that she didn't have a right to hold the child she'd loved and raised. Cooper eased Liam from Linda's arms, kissed his cheek and held him for a few precious seconds before he passed him to Jessa so she could do the same.

She did.

But then she burst into tears.

"It's okay," he tried to assure her, and he lowered his head, intending to give her a reassuring peck on the forehead. Too many nicks there, so he just went for her mouth.

And Cooper really kissed her. Long, slow and deep.

Jessa didn't stop him, either. She just melted into the kiss as if they were the only people on the ranch. It went on for so long that Tucker cleared his throat, reminding him that they weren't alone.

"Why don't you go ahead and take Jessa, Liam and Linda back to the house?" Colt suggested. "Tucker and I can tie up loose ends here. I've already called the doc and he's on the way. Looks like he'll need to do some stitching up."

Yes, there were cuts on Jessa's face and arms, each one of them an angry reminder of how bad things had gotten. And how much worse they could have been.

Cooper thanked both his brothers, not just for handling the loose ends but for everything they'd done tonight. And not done. They hadn't made a fuss about him kissing Jessa.

Cooper got Jessa, Liam and Linda into Colt's truck and started the short drive to the house. It was so quiet, you could almost hear a pin drop, and that was when Liam woke up. His eyes popped open and he sat up, looking first at Jessa.

"Mama," he said, smiling. He snuggled into her arms as if he might go back to sleep. Then he spotted the cuts on her head and frowned. "Got bad boo-boos." And he lifted his shirt to show her the bandage from his surgery.

"Mama's fine," she whispered, her voice surprisingly calm. "Grandma and Daddy are, too."

Liam's gaze went from Linda to Cooper. He stayed quiet a moment, as if trying to figure out why Jessa had called him the *D* word, and he gave Cooper a hard once-over.

"Daddy's got boo-boos," he said.

Good thing Cooper hadn't been standing, or his legs might have buckled. It was the first time his son had called him Daddy, and it wouldn't be the last. *Daddy* was something he'd never tire of hearing.

Cooper stopped the truck directly in front of the house and got them inside. Away from the chaos that was about to happen with the arrival of the medical examiner and his crew.

However, there was a crew of a different kind inside.

Roy, Rosalie and Arlene were all in the foyer waiting. Rayanne was at the top of the stairs, and she glanced at each of them and must have

decided the danger was over and that a famil
moment was to follow. She turned, heading bac
toward her room.

"Thank God you're all right," his father said
and Arlene and Rosalie echoed the same.

Rosalie gave Liam a quick checkup, but the
shook her head when she examined Jessa an
Cooper. "You both need to see the doctor."

"We will." But not right now. Now he wante
to deal with the aftermath.

Maybe the future, too.

"I need a long soak in the tub," Linda said
making her way up the stairs. "Maybe a shot c
Jack Daniel's."

"I'll bring some up to you," Arlene offered
"Could use a drink or two myself." She made
face when she looked at Cooper's arm. "If that'
the worst of it, then I guess we made out all right.

Yeah, they had. Partly because of luck an
partly because of help from Jessa and his family
Together, they'd kept Liam safe and all but Pegg
alive. Excluding her, everyone who counted wa
in one piece.

"Want me to take Liam?" Rosalie offered.

Jessa and Cooper jumped to say no. Coope
figured it would be a while before they let hin
out of their sight. Rosalie smiled and excuse
herself.

His father and Arlene gave Cooper knowin

looks. Which was strange. Since he wasn't sure how the next few minutes would play out. Cooper only knew these would be some of the most important minutes of his life.

With Liam still in Jessa's arms, they went upstairs to the guest room. When Liam saw his crib, he motioned to get in it, but Cooper soon realized it was just to play with the toy horse on top of the covers. Cooper made a mental note to get him more toy horses.

A real one, too.

While he was at it, he went through the rest of his mental notes, which started with Jessa. Except she spoke before he could.

"I'll move in with you," she said.

Okay. That was a good start, but Cooper wanted a heck of a lot more. "You told Liam I was his daddy."

She nodded, swallowed hard. "Because you are. He needs you, Cooper." Another nod, and her gaze cautiously came to his. "I need you."

The corner of his mouth lifted. That definitely qualified as more. Cooper eased his arm around her, brought her to him and kissed her. It didn't go on nearly as long as he wanted. Of course, a lifetime might not be long enough. But Jessa broke the kiss and looked up at him.

"We still have things to work out," she said. "With your mother's trial, for instance."

Yeah, that. "I don't see a way around it. You'll have to excuse yourself as prosecuting attorney or else someone could claim a conflict of interest." He eased her back to him. "And just in case you're wondering, there will be a conflict."

He kissed her to show her just how much of one there'd be. Like the kiss in the pasture, it went on a little too long, and Liam started to laugh.

"Mama and Daddy kiss-kiss." And he got in on it by leaning out from his crib and motioning for them to kiss him.

They did.

The moment was perfect, but it didn't last. Jessa got that pained look on her face again. "What I said back there is true. I know I'll never be able to replace Molly."

Well, Jessa was certainly hitting the high points, things that definitely needed a clearing of the air.

"I don't want you to replace her. Molly will always be here." He tapped his heart. "And here." Cooper ran his hand over Liam's hair. "You're your own woman. And you're Liam's mom."

"Daddy," Liam proudly announced.

"Yeah, I am." And Cooper hoped to be a lot more when it came to Jessa and his son.

The tears came, watering Jessa's eyes. Maybe because she had expected him to tell her what he'd figured out after nearly losing both of them to a madman.

"I'm in love with you," he said.

He wasn't a man who said the words easily, but they came easily tonight. Clarity had a way of doing that, of boiling everything down so that Cooper could see what was most important.

And what was most important was in this room with him.

"I'm in love with you, too," Jessa said, but then she shook her head, almost as if in disgust. "But love doesn't make it easier. Your family—"

He kissed her to cut that off. And because he just wanted to feel her mouth on his. "My family will accept you just fine. Now, let's go back to that other part that you rushed right over. The part about you loving me."

She nodded. "I do love you."

"I wove you," Liam piped in, causing them to laugh. Liam obviously enjoyed their reaction, because he started repeating it.

Cooper gave his son a kiss on the cheek. "I'm going to ask your mama to marry me." There was no way Liam could have known what that meant, but he smiled, anyway. "Should she say yes?"

Liam bobbed his head. "Yesss."

With that seal of approval, Cooper turned back

to Jessa, waiting for her to answer. But he didn't have to wait at all. She landed right in his arms.

"Yes," she said. "Yes, yes, a thousand times, yes."

That was the exact answer Cooper had wanted to hear. He kissed her, hard and long. Then he gathered up Liam and kissed her again.

Finally, Cooper had everything that he wanted right in his arms.

* * * * *

USA TODAY *bestselling author
Delores Fossen's new miniseries,*
SWEETWATER RANCH,
*is just getting started.
Look for* COWBOY WITH A BADGE
*next month, wherever Harlequin Intrigue
books are sold!*

LARGER-PRINT BOOKS!
GET 2 FREE LARGER-PRINT NOVELS PLUS
2 FREE GIFTS!

❤ HARLEQUIN®

Romance

From the Heart, For the Heart

YES! Please send me 2 FREE LARGER-PRINT Harlequin® Romance novels and my 2 FREE gifts (gifts are worth about $10). After receiving them, if I don't wish to receive any more books, I can return the shipping statement marked "cancel." If I don't cancel, I will receive 4 brand-new novels every month and be billed just $4.84 per book in the U.S. or $5.24 per book in Canada. That's a savings of at least 19% off the cover price! It's quite a bargain! Shipping and handling is just 50¢ per book in the U.S. and 75¢ per book in Canada.* I understand that accepting the 2 free books and gifts places me under no obligation to buy anything. I can always return a shipment and cancel at any time. Even if I never buy another book, the two free books and gifts are mine to keep forever.

119/319 HDN F43Y

Name	(PLEASE PRINT)

Address		Apt. #

City	State/Prov.	Zip/Postal Code

Signature (if under 18, a parent or guardian must sign)

Mail to the **Harlequin® Reader Service:**
IN U.S.A.: P.O. Box 1867, Buffalo, NY 14240-1867
IN CANADA: P.O. Box 609, Fort Erie, Ontario L2A 5X3

Want to try two free books from another line?
Call 1-800-873-8635 or visit www.ReaderService.com.

* Terms and prices subject to change without notice. Prices do not include applicable taxes. Sales tax applicable in N.Y. Canadian residents will be charged applicable taxes. Offer not valid in Quebec. This offer is limited to one order per household. Not valid for current subscribers to Harlequin Romance Larger-Print books. All orders subject to credit approval. Credit or debit balances in a customer's account(s) may be offset by any other outstanding balance owed by or to the customer. Please allow 4 to 6 weeks for delivery. Offer available while quantities last.

Your Privacy—The Harlequin® Reader Service is committed to protecting your privacy. Our Privacy Policy is available online at www.ReaderService.com or upon request from the Harlequin Reader Service.

We make a portion of our mailing list available to reputable third parties that offer products we believe may interest you. If you prefer that we not exchange your name with third parties, or if you wish to clarify or modify your communication preferences, please visit us at www.ReaderService.com/consumerchoice or write to us at Harlequin Reader Service Preference Service, P.O. Box 9062, Buffalo, NY 14269. Include your complete name and address.

HRLP13R

ReaderService.com

Manage your account online!

- Review your order history
- Manage your payments
- Update your address

---

*We've designed
the Harlequin® Reader Service
website just for you.*

Enjoy all the features!

- Reader excerpts from any series
- Respond to mailings and special monthly offers
- Discover new series available to you
- Browse the Bonus Bucks catalog
- Share your feedback

Visit us at:

ReaderService.com